"Can I have Neesha's seat, Mr. Cloverhill? I can't see the board very well."

The voice belonged to T.J. Miller. Neesha Patel was absent that day.

The hairs on the back of my neck stood on end as T.J. slid into the seat behind me. I gripped my pen and stared at the chalkboard, the words swimming before my eyes.

"Nobody believed me about you," T.J. whispered, the sound of his voice making my heart lurch. "But they believe me now," he added softly. "Now that they've read all about you in the newspaper."

I forced myself to ignore him, and tried to focus on what Mr. Cloverhill was saying.

"Willa Cather was a literary trailblazer on the American scene." As Mr. Cloverhill continued his lecture, I felt a finger run softly down the nape of my neck.

Startled, I dropped my pen on the floor. I was sure that every pair of eyes in the classroom was on me, and when the bell rang, I leaped to my feet and practically knocked over the girl in front of me.

By the time I got to my locker, I was choking back

**3**

# TURNING
## seventeen

## For Real

### by Christa Roberts

A PARACHUTE PRESS BOOK

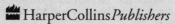 HarperCollins*Publishers*

Created and produced by
PARACHUTE PUBLISHING, L.L.C.
156 Fifth Avenue, Suite 302
New York, NY 10010

*PAYA*
*R6435fo*

Published by
HarperCollins*Publishers*
1350 Avenue of the Americas
New York, NY 10019

First HarperCollins*Publishers* printing, October 2000

HarperCollins® and 📖®
are trademarks of HarperCollins*Publishers*, Inc.

Library of Congress Catalog Card Number: 00-100946
ISBN 0-06-447239-6

Printed in the U.S.A.

10 9 8 7 6 5 4 3 2 1

Design by AFF Design
Cover photos by Anna Palma
Hair and makeup by Julie Matos for Oribe Salon

# For Real

# Chapter 1

I opened my eyes and sat up, blinking and rubbing my stiff neck. *What time is it?* I wondered.

I straightened my cramped legs, which stuck to the leather on the backseat of my BMW, and stared groggily out the window. I had spent the night in my car. I'd parked it on the University of Wisconsin campus, crawled into the backseat, and fallen asleep.

A couple of college girls walked by, clutching Styrofoam coffee cups. It must be Saturday morning, I realized. A sick feeling washed over me. I'd slept in my car because I couldn't face going home. And now that I'd stayed out all night, going home would be even worse.

Everything at home just felt wrong. My mother was gone. She had died of ovarian cancer almost two years ago, and I still thought about her all the time. I missed her. I *needed* her. So many weird things were happening to me, and I didn't really know how to handle them.

My dad wasn't much help. Ever since Mom died, he'd kind of pulled away from me. He was a district attorney, and for the last couple of years he'd been working harder than ever. He was so overprotective of me, I felt as if I couldn't breathe sometimes. And I couldn't really talk to him. He never had time.

And then there was T.J.

At the beginning of our senior year, my friend Kerri Hopkins had made it her mission to help me find a boyfriend. I felt a little embarrassed about it, but all of my friends had boyfriends, and I was feeling left out. Jessica Carvelli had been with her boyfriend, Alex, since tenth grade. Erin Yamada had fallen madly in love with a guy named Keith in Seattle and was having a long-distance relationship, mostly through e-mail. And Kerri could get any guy she wanted, including Matt Fowler, the star of the football team.

I guess it was a little pathetic—I was a senior, and I'd never had a boyfriend. I'd never even kissed a boy—not really. For one thing, my dad thought I was too young to date—he said he wouldn't let me date until college. I was almost a year younger than the rest of my class, and I was shy. I wasn't funny like Erin or a genius like Jessica or gorgeous like Kerri. My mom was from Argentina, and I inherited her features: long, straight dark hair, brown eyes, olive skin, high cheekbones, and a wide, full mouth. But somehow my mom was a beauty and I wasn't.

Anyway, Kerri kept after me. She asked me who I thought was cute and I told her: T.J. Miller. "He's perfect for you," Kerri agreed. "You're both athletic, so you'll have a lot in common." I played field hockey, and T.J. was on the basketball team. "And he doesn't have a girlfriend," she added.

Kerri, Jessica, and Erin pushed me to talk to T.J. and smile at him in the halls, stuff like that. At first, he didn't seem interested.

Then this football player named Turtle had a party after a big game, and we all went. I felt so happy when T.J. started talking to me at the party. I thought Kerri's plan must be working.

At school I'd always felt tongue-tied around him, but now he was easy to talk to. He listened closely to everything I said, and we really did seem to have a lot in common.

After a while we went downstairs into the basement to check out Turtle's large-screen TV. The volume was blasting, so T.J. suggested we go into the den so we could talk. When we got there, he started kissing me, hard. At first I kissed him back, but then I felt like things were getting out of hand. I didn't want to be uncool, so I just said, "T.J., slow down."

3

He wouldn't. He kept kissing me and pawing me. I said he was going too far, that he had to stop. "Deal with it," he said.

I couldn't make him quit. His hands were everywhere. I started to run out of the den, but he grabbed my arm and threw me down on the couch. I was terrified. He ripped my shirt before I managed to push him away and run out of the room.

T.J.'s assault didn't end there. He started telling all of his friends that we had slept together. Whenever I saw him and his friends at school, they said horrible things to me. Things like, "You did it with T.J., so will you do it with us? We heard you really like it."

I wanted to run and hide every time I saw them. I hated going to school. I stayed home whenever I could, telling my dad I felt sick. I wasn't doing much studying lately, either. I'd always been a good student, but suddenly I just didn't care.

So now here I was sitting in my car, trying to figure out where to go. I was starving. I hadn't had anything to eat since that awful hot dog at South Central's homecoming game last night.

The homecoming game—another disaster. I didn't even want to go, but it was a big night for my three best friends. Erin was homecoming queen, Kerri was a cheerleader, and Jessica was a court princess. So I was sitting in the bleachers by myself. This guy Luke Perez sat down and started talking to me. I knew Luke a little, and he seemed like a nice guy. But then again, T.J. had seemed nice too.

All Luke did was lightly touch my shoulder—and I snapped. I jumped up and ran away before he could say another word.

I got into the BMW and drove for hours around the streets of Madison. And I ended up here, in Parking Lot C at the University of Wisconsin. I knew I should go home, but I just couldn't bring myself to do it. I felt so confused and guilty, and there was no one at home to help me. No one could help me with what bothered me most.

Deep down I wondered if the whole thing with T.J. wasn't my fault. Had I led him on somehow? Had I done something to make him act like that?

I turned the key in the ignition, and the BMW's engine hummed. I wasn't ready to face my dad, but I could go to Kerri's. I knew I could count on her.

Thirty minutes later Kerri flung open the door to her apartment, dragged me inside, and threw her arms around me.

"Where have you been? We were so worried!" Kerri dragged me into the kitchen. Erin and Jessica jumped to their feet when they saw me.

"Maya! Are you all right?" Jessica cried.

"Where have you been?" Erin demanded.

"I'm sorry," I said, feeling sheepish. "I was just driving around."

"All night?" Jessica said.

"Well, I parked at the university. I slept in my car."

They stared at me in shock. "You *slept* in your *car*?" Erin repeated.

"I . . . I just couldn't go home," I admitted.

"Maya, your father came to my house this morning, looking for you," Jessica said. "He's really upset."

Kerri picked up the phone. "You've got to call him," she insisted.

"I know," I said, biting my lip. "I'm just not ready yet. What am I going to say to him? He's going to kill me!"

"Maya!" Kerri shook the phone at me. "You have to call."

"Look, Ker, don't make me call him just yet," I pleaded. "I've got to decide what to tell him."

Kerri sighed. "Fine. You want some breakfast first? Will that give you some courage?"

"I hope so," I replied. Jessica, Erin, and I sat down at the table while Kerri made her famous waffles.

"We're really worried about you, girl," Erin said.

"You can't go on like this," Jessica added. "Missing school, staying in bed all day, not caring about anything. And we . . ." She paused and looked at Kerri and Erin. "We don't know how to help you. This whole thing has kind of spiraled out of control."

"I know," I whispered.

"Spending the day in bed is one thing," Kerri put in. "But spending the night in a parking lot?" She dropped into the chair next to me. "Maybe you should talk to someone. You know, my mom could give you a referral to a therapist if you want."

Liz Hopkins, Kerri's mom, was a guidance counselor at a junior high school. I knew she meant well. But the idea of telling a total stranger all of my problems made my stomach hurt.

I shook my head, blinking back tears. "I'm not going to a shrink. And I don't think my dad would like it."

"Maya, your dad already knows something is seriously wrong," Jessica said. "You didn't go home last night."

Kerri set a plate of waffles in front of me. I stared at it, suddenly not hungry anymore.

*Maybe if I did have someone to talk to,* I thought, *someone I could open up to who would be impartial, who didn't know any of the people at South Central. . . .*

*Maybe that would make me feel a little less confused.*

"Maya! I'm so glad you're all right." Liz Hopkins walked into the room, dressed in a mauve bodysuit and gray leggings. She came over to me and squeezed my shoulder. "You gave us all a scare." She glanced at the phone. "Please tell me you've called your dad to let him know you're safe."

I shrugged, embarrassed. "No, not yet."

Liz shook her head, her lips pinched together. "You have to call your father. Or let me, if it's easier."

"Could you call?" Then I hesitated. "Um, Liz, I was thinking. . . ." I took a breath and summoned all my courage. "Could you, um, that is, would you be willing to give me the name of someone who maybe I could talk to?"

"Say no more." Liz picked up a writing tablet and scribbled down a name. "Valerie Sheridan. She's very good and very nice. You'll like her."

I took the piece of paper she handed me and started for the door. "Please tell my dad I'm on my way home."

The automatic yard sprinklers were coming on as I unlocked our massive front door and tiptoed into the foyer. My friends and I called the big, cold, empty house where I lived "the castle." As usual, everything looked immaculate and smelled of lemons. The castle is a decorator's dream, but not exactly cozy. I missed our old small, suburban house in Kensington Heights, where I grew up with Erin, Jessica, and Kerri. When I told Erin we were moving to a minimansion near Lake Monona, she shrieked with glee. "You're so lucky!" she cried. "Those houses are gorgeous!"

I didn't feel lucky. I didn't like the cold marble floors or the spotless white living room out of *Architectural Digest*. And Dad and I didn't really need four bathrooms.

My dad rushed toward me from the living room and gave me a quick, hard hug. "Maya! Are you all right?"

I nodded. "I'm fine. Really."

"Where on earth were you all night? I was worried sick. I was just about to call the police."

"I . . . I was just driving around," I stammered. "I felt kind of confused . . . and I parked and fell asleep in the car."

I saw relief in his blue eyes, then a flash of anger. "Into my study. Now."

Silently I followed him, cringing as my eyes met Betty's. Betty was our housekeeper who worked from nine to four. She made sure that Dad and I had a well-balanced diet, and she kept our house neat as a pin.

Once inside the study, Dad sat down at his desk

and leaned back, his forehead creased. "Maya, I'm confused. You've always been so levelheaded. What got into you?" He shook his head. "Why would you do something like that?"

My mouth felt dry. I wished I could tell him about T.J. and how horrible I felt. But I couldn't. "I don't know, Dad," I mumbled. "I guess I've just been having a hard time lately."

"What you did is very serious, Maya. I'm afraid I'll have to ground you."

I wasn't thrilled about being grounded. But then I thought, what difference did it make? There was nowhere I really wanted to go, anyway.

*And at least I know he cares about me*, I thought. *I guess that's better than nothing.*

Then he cleared his throat. "Enough about that. I need to talk to you, Maya. You know I'm going to be running for lieutenant governor."

I nodded. My dad had been meeting with political consultants for weeks. Our house was like a zoo sometimes, filled with advisors and lawyers and other bores in khakis and button-down shirts.

"Next week I'll officially toss my hat into the ring," Dad told me. "I'll be making a formal announcement."

"Wow, Dad. That's terrific," I said, not sure how I really felt. Life in the castle would be even more of a pressure cooker than ever—that I knew for sure.

"It's going to be a rough campaign," my father went on. "I'll need to be able to rely on you, Maya. No more stunts like last night. The press is going to be watching me—and my family—very closely."

"I'm sorry," I said, and I meant it. I slipped my hand into my pocket and felt the piece of paper with the therapist's name and number that Kerri's mother had given me.

I took a deep breath. "I won't ever do that again, Dad, I promise," I said. "But Dad—I need help. I need someone to talk to. To help me deal with stuff."

"If you're having problems, Maya, you can come to me anytime."

"I know, but . . ." This was hard for me to say. "I think I need more than that. Liz Hopkins gave me the name of a therapist. She's supposed to be very good."

"A therapist?" my dad echoed.

I showed him the paper with Dr. Sheridan's name on it.

My dad studied the paper, frowning. He didn't say anything for a long time.

"Dad?" I asked. "What do you think? Can I call her?"

Dad crumpled the paper and tossed it into the trash can. "No," he said. "Absolutely not."

# Chapter 2

■ couldn't believe it. How could my father refuse to let me get help?

"Dad—why not?" I asked him, blinking back tears.

"Maya, I'm in a delicate position here. If people found out that my daughter was in therapy . . . well, they might get the wrong impression. The press could use it against me." His expression softened when he noticed the tears in my eyes. He reached into the trash can and pulled out the piece of paper.

"I'm sorry, Maya," he said, handing it back to me. "I shouldn't have reacted that way." He paused. "I'll tell you what. After the election, you can see a therapist if you still want to. Is that fair?"

I swallowed. I didn't want to do anything to hurt my father's campaign. I nodded.

"Good. Now why don't you go up to your room and clean yourself up."

"Okay, Dad," I said.

I trudged upstairs and threw myself on my bed. I didn't get up again all day.

The next morning, Sunday, I grabbed some clothes off the pile in the bottom of my closet and shuffled downstairs to the kitchen.

A harried-looking guy in a white oxford shirt sat hunched over the kitchen table. "Did you get that tax reform folder?" he asked me without looking up.

"Huh?" I said.

He glanced up and squinted at me. "Oh, Maya, it's you. Sorry." He hurried into the dining room, where my dad sat at the table surrounded by newspapers, faxes, his chief assistant, Peter Fontana, a couple of attorneys, and Marlene Carroll, a public relations person for a child advocacy group. Her daughter, Amanda, went to South Central, but she was a sophomore. I didn't really know her.

I helped myself to a glass of juice and a doughnut from a box on the kitchen counter. The campaign buzz was going strong. They were all getting revved up for my dad's big announcement. Still half asleep, I felt like a visitor from another planet.

"I'm expecting a hand-delivered package from Greg Watson by ten-thirty," my father was saying. He was dressed for work in dark slacks and a dress shirt, his silk tie flipped over his shoulder. "He's worked up some figures for the day care program. I want to present them when I announce my candidacy." He skimmed the *Madison Herald* and then the business section of the *New York Times*. Poor Dad. He couldn't even relax on Sunday morning.

"Morning," I said. I shifted uncomfortably from one foot to the other. Kerri had called earlier to see if I could meet her at Bernie's Bagels, the bagel place where she worked. She had a long shift on Sunday and wanted some company. She also said that Jessica had broken up with Alex, at least for now, and would be there too. I told her Dad had grounded me, but she begged me to ask him anyway.

My father's clear blue eyes peered at me over the top of the paper. "Morning, sweetheart." Then he turned back to Peter. "If I get a fax from George Green, make sure to page me."

Marlene suddenly noticed me. She looked me over. "Spencer, I think we're going to need to do something about Maya's, um . . . look," she said.

Marlene had practically taken Dad over since she joined his campaign team. She acted as if *she* was his chief adviser, not Peter.

"Hmmm . . . what?" my dad said, not really listening to her.

I glanced down at my old jeans with the holes in the knees, my not-quite-clean T-shirt, and beat-up dirty sneakers. What was wrong with my look? I shrugged at Marlene, then cleared my throat. "So, Dad . . ." I began.

"Friday night's fund-raiser was terrific," my father told me, picking up the cordless phone. "We raised almost three hundred grand for the campaign. Combined with the one we did last month in Eau Claire, we're in fine shape."

"That's great," I said.

"Did you see how that society snob Felicity Waters was carrying on?" one of the other attorneys broke in. "You had Madison's wealthiest woman eating out of your hand!"

My dad smiled. "Never met a contributor I didn't like." They began talking about some of the other guests at the fund-raiser, and Dad seemed to forget that I was in the room.

"Dad," I interrupted. "I'm going to go pick up Erin and drive down to Bernie's to see Kerri. Okay?"

I braced myself for an explosion. What Dad says, goes. And Dad had said I was grounded.

But he just flashed a quick smile at me and clicked on the phone. "Good, sweetie. Enjoy." He pressed a button and said, "Bob! Spencer Greer here. Now, about that family leave plan . . ."

*Did he forget?* I wondered, fighting back the lump that was forming in my throat. *Doesn't he care?*

I gulped down my juice, tossed the doughnut, and headed back upstairs to my room. A little while later I left the house without even bothering to say good-bye.

I drove to Erin's house to pick her up.

"How are you doing, Maya?" Erin tossed her Josie & the Pussycats lunchbox purse on the floor of my car and hopped in.

"All hail Queen Erin!" I bowed slightly. She gave me a stiff homecoming-queen wave, as if she was sitting on top of a float. "It's an honor to drive you, Your Majesty."

Erin batted her long eyelashes. "Ah, yes, my adoring public awaits me at Bernie's."

She didn't look much like a homecoming queen that morning. She wore faded jeans with crystals dripping from the hems, a vintage black top, and green suede loafers. Her dark hair was pencil straight, and she had on thick-rimmed black glasses. Erin tried a new look almost every week. She dyed her hair different colors, wore different styles of clothes. . . . I admired the way she followed her moods.

"You amaze me," I told her. "You're the chameleon of South Central High."

Erin looked through the CDs in my travel case. "Change can be good," she said. "Maybe *you* could make some changes, Maya."

I struck a pose behind the wheel. "Yeah, baby. I think I should go for the glam look."

She frowned. "No, I'm serious. You need to speak to somebody about this . . ." She paused, fumbling for the right word. ". . . this funk you've been in lately. Are you going to call the therapist?"

I bit my lip. "I wish I could, Erin. It's just . . . " I thought about Dad and how he didn't want me to see a therapist during his campaign. How could I tell Erin about that? "It's too complicated. Can we talk about something else?"

"Sure. Sorry." She held up a CD and when I nodded, she slid it into the CD player.

"So how's Keith?" I asked, trying to change the subject.

Erin played with her belt loop. "Fine, as far as I know. But all I've gotten from him lately are forwarded jokes on e-mail. They're funny, but . . . we don't talk as much lately," she confessed. "Only about once a week now."

"I'm sure he's thinking about you all the time," I said. "And wait till he hears about homecoming!"

Erin slumped down in the gray leather seat. "Yeah, I know. And don't get me wrong, I'm really

**17**

happy that I won and all that, but . . ." She shrugged. "It's just that Keith and I were so close. I don't know. Maybe I'm just being paranoid, but I think things may be changing between us, and I don't know how to fix it."

She reached for the volume knob on the CD player and turned up the music. "I love this song," she shouted, bopping her head. When it was over, she turned the volume down and said, "I do have some good news from Seattle."

"What?" I asked.

"My aunt Joyce is getting married!"

I grinned. "That's great!" Erin loved her aunt Joyce. She was young and cool, more like a friend to Erin than an aunt.

I pulled into Bernie's parking lot and took the last space.

The bagel shop was packed with people from South Central and tons of University of Wisconsin students. This was the place to be on Sundays.

Erin and I bought coffee and bagels and maneuvered our way between the tables and chairs.

"Hey, Erin." Two members of the football team— Jorge Rivera and Tim Gardner—smiled at Erin from their seats. They didn't seem to see me.

"Hi." Erin grinned at them, then flashed me a look that said, "What's this about?" Neither of us knew Jorge and Tim very well—they were too popular.

"What are you up to?" Tim asked.

"I'll go get us a table," I said to Erin. I found an empty table and glanced over at Erin. Tim and Jorge were definitely flirting with her.

"Can you believe it?" she said when she joined me a few minutes later. "Tim Gardner and Jorge Rivera—who have never even said hello to me before—were practically kissing my feet." She dropped into her chair. "What's up with that?"

I shrugged. "It must be because you're the homecoming queen. Being royalty is bound to have benefits."

Erin sniffed. "I don't need that kind of attention." She looked around. "There's Kerri." Kerri waved and headed toward us, clutching a latte.

"Guys!" Kerri said, grinning as she joined us. "You should have waited for me—I could have sneaked you some free coffee."

Erin scooted over so Kerri could squeeze in. "How's it going?"

Kerri plucked a piece of muffin from her burgundy Bernie's polo shirt. "Do you have any idea how much cream cheese people eat? I feel like we've served the entire population of Wisconsin today. I mean, they don't have to take our rep as the cheese capital of the world so seriously."

"Hey—look at that guy," Erin said under her breath as a guy with bulging muscles sat down next to us and dove into the first of three egg-and-cheese bagel sandwiches.

"Eww! He's neckless," Kerri said, shuddering.

"There's Jessica," Erin said, looking up at the coffee bar. Jessica was leaning against the wall, talking to Alex. She wore her long, wavy brown hair in a ponytail.

"Yo! Jess!" Kerri yelled.

"Do you think she wants to be interrupted?" I whispered.

Jessica turned our way and waved. We watched as she kissed Alex good-bye on the cheek and made her way to our table. "Hi, guys," she said, dropping into a seat.

"What's the deal with you and Alex?" Erin asked.

"You guys are looking cozy again," Kerri said.

Jessica shrugged. "It's weird. I mean, we just broke up yesterday, so it doesn't feel real. We're kind of hanging out."

Kerri stirred her latte. "You're right. That is weird."

"Maybe Alex wants to get back together again," I suggested. "He obviously still cares about you."

"I know he does. But we both need some time,"

Jessica said. "It's funny, though. My heart kind of races when I see him. Especially when he wears that old leather jacket."

I turned to see what she meant. But instead, my gaze fell on a guy at the counter dressed in jeans and a UW sweatshirt, a backward Green Bay baseball cap on his head, dark wavy hair curling out at the edges.

It was Luke Perez. Here, in Bernie's. He had a paper sack in front of him, and he was with two other guys I recognized from school, but whose names I didn't know. I watched, beads of sweat breaking out on my forehead, as he paid for his food. What was he doing here? Was it a coincidence—or had he followed me?

"He's here," I whispered, slinking down in my seat. Everywhere I turned lately, Luke popped up. And he always seemed to be staring at me. Not staring in a bad way, more like he was curious, like he wanted to find out more about me.

But I wasn't going to let him.

"Who's here?" Kerri asked, eyes wide. "T.J.?"

I shook my head, trying to move my lips as little as possible. "Luke. Don't look."

"Luke Perez?" Erin exclaimed, her eyes darting around.

"Where?" Jessica asked, craning her neck so much the couple at the table in front of us actually ducked out of the way.

"Geez, be obvious, you guys!" I whispered, wanting to die. I was afraid their staring would make Luke think I liked him—and I didn't.

"Ooh, there he is," Kerri said, zeroing in. "And he looks cute." She smiled encouragingly. "Just like he always does."

I shook my head. "Kerri, please don't start. I told you. I'm not interested in going out with anyone. I mean it."

Kerri reached over and patted my hand. "Don't get mad, Maya. It's just that Luke seems really nice. I don't want you to miss out on something good just because of T.J."

"Alex knows Luke a little. He says he's a good guy," Jessica put in.

Erin leaned toward me, her shiny black hair framing her face. "I heard Luke's mom died a few years ago, Maya. It's kind of morbid, I guess, but you guys would have that in common."

I grimaced. "Wow, a match made in heaven." I pretended to be very interested in my bagel. But then, for the first time since I'd noticed him, I allowed myself a peek. He was tall and broad-shouldered, and his wavy dark hair reached the nape of his neck. His cheekbones were high and his eyes were dark. I liked how they seemed to smile when he talked with his friends.

To my horror, Luke looked right at me. For a moment it was as if we were the only two people in Bernie's. Luke started to smile, and I almost thought he was going to come over to our table. Then, almost shyly, he looked away.

Of course, my friends had witnessed the whole thing.

"Maya, please don't get upset," Kerri said softly. "But I think Luke really likes you. I know you're not ready for anything heavy, but could you try to be open to *something*?"

I shook my head. "Okay, he's cute. But that's what I thought about T.J., and look where that got me."

Erin scowled into her latte. "That guy is a bad dream."

Without realizing what I was doing, I let my eyes travel back up to the counter where I'd seen Luke. He was gone.

Well, that was fine by me. Because there was no way I would ever go out with Luke, or any other guy. Just because someone seemed nice on the outside didn't mean he was nice on the inside.

"Hey." Two guys wearing varsity jackets stopped by our table. I vaguely recognized them.

The taller guy, a lanky blond dressed in head-to-toe Tommy Hilfiger, spoke to Erin. "That's really cool about homecoming."

His friend, a shorter, fatter guy with a buzz cut, grinned. "You totally deserved it. We voted for you."

Erin seemed slightly embarrassed. "Uh, thanks, guys." She gave them a smile as they sauntered away, then turned back to us, her brow wrinkled. "Who *are* these people?"

Kerri reached over and poked her in the ribs. "You're getting a lot of attention all of a sudden," she said. She grinned at Erin. "You know, it can't hurt to have a little fun with this."

Erin buried her face in her hands. "No, it *can*. Talking to all of these guys just makes me miss Keith even more! Keith is smart, sweet, and sexy, all rolled into one."

Jessica held up a finger. "You left one more 's' word out—Seattle."

"Don't remind me." Erin sighed.

"Listen," Kerri said. "You told me you're afraid things are cooling off between you and Keith. So why not test the relationship a little? It can't hurt to go out with a few other guys and see how you like them."

"And if you don't like them, you'll know Keith is really the one," Jessica said.

"Besides, Keith never has to know," Kerri added. "There are some advantages to having a boyfriend in Seattle, after all."

Erin looked unsure. "I guess it couldn't hurt," she said. "But I already think Keith is the one!"

"This way you'll find out for sure," Jessica coaxed.

Erin glanced around the room at all the guys who were looking at her. "It *is* kind of tempting."

A guy in a Westdale High jacket, who was sitting at the table next to us, suddenly leaned over and tugged on Erin's sleeve. "Hey. Isn't your name Erin?"

Kerri rolled her eyes and stood up. "Duty calls."

"Yeah, I've got to get back to the books," Jessica said. "Alex is going to give me a ride to the library." She gathered her things and headed for Alex's table.

I tapped Erin on the shoulder. She was now in deep conversation with the Westdale guy. "Hey, Er, I'm kind of ready to go."

Erin made a face. "But we just got here!"

"Don't make her leave," the Westdale guy begged.

Kerri laughed. "If you want to hang out another hour, Erin, you can catch a ride with me."

"It's a deal," Erin said, then she looked up at me. "Are you sure it's okay, Maya?" she asked. "I mean, I can leave with you if you want."

"I'm fine," I assured her. "I just feel like going home."

I said my good-byes, grabbed my purse, and

made my way through the crowd.

It felt good to be back outside in the fresh air. As I crossed South Street and headed toward the parking lot, a familiar voice called out my name.

"Maya! Maya, wait up!"

My spine stiffened. It was T.J. Miller.

# *Chapter 3*

I quickened my pace. I didn't dare turn around. The sound of sneakers thumping the pavement behind me sent a lump of terror into my throat.

"Yo, Maya! I knew it was you." T.J. jogged up beside me, his eyes bright. "No one else wears a pair of jeans like you."

My stomach churned as he looked down at my car keys. I fought to keep my hands from shaking.

"I've missed you," he said softly.

"Missed me?" I managed to repeat, not slowing my steps. My car was only about fifty feet away. If I could only get there . . .

"Hey, do you think I could catch a ride?" he asked casually. "I walked here, and I'm pretty beat."

"No," I blurted out. "No, I, uh, have to get home right away. My dad's expecting me."

T.J. cleared his throat. "You know, Maya, it

27

doesn't have to be like this. I got it, okay? You like to play hard to get. That's cool. But enough's enough, right?" He reached over and gently squeezed my shoulder.

Just the thought of him touching me nauseated me. I jerked my shoulder away. "Leave me alone," I said stiffly as we reached my car. I hesitated, gripping the keys in my sweaty hand. I couldn't wait to get safely inside the car. But what if he forced his way inside too? My muscles tensed. I had to move quickly.

Just then a man carrying his small daughter came up to the minivan next to my car. They smiled over at us. Here was my chance—and I took it. I pushed Unlock on my key chain. Then I whipped open the door, and dove into the driver's seat, slamming the door and simultaneously locking it in three seconds flat.

Shoving the keys into the ignition, I yanked the gear into reverse and flew out of the parking spot. T.J. had to jump away to avoid getting his left foot run over. Without a backward glance I peeled out toward the exit and onto the street.

My hands were sweaty and shaking. I was so nervous I could hardly see.

I pulled over to the curb and rested my head on the steering wheel, catching my breath.

*I can't take this anymore*, I thought. *Always*

*looking over my shoulder. Panicking every time I see T.J. What if he forces himself on me again—and I can't get away?*

I was desperate. I felt as if I had to talk to somebody or I'd go crazy.

I reached into my purse and pulled out the now-crumpled piece of paper Liz Hopkins had given me. With shaking fingers, I punched the therapist's number into my cell phone, holding the paper like a lifeline.

"Um, hi. My name is Maya Greer, and I was wondering if I could set up a time to come and talk to you in your office. Because I really think I need some help. . . ."

# Chapter 4

**I**'m so glad you phoned Dr. Sheridan," Kerri told me as we walked down the hall on Monday morning.

"My dad is going to explode if he finds out," I admitted. "Anyway, my first session is tomorrow after school."

I sighed. With T.J. and his friends bothering me, school was a nightmare. But outside of school was almost as bad. Marlene had turned the castle into Makeover Central. As soon as she saw me this morning she sized up what I was wearing, criticized it, and just happened to have something "more appropriate" on hand for me to try. The night before she'd handed me a newspaper, told me to read it, and then quizzed me on campaign issues, "just to see" how I'd answer.

"I'm kind of nervous about seeing Dr. Sheridan," I admitted to Kerri. "But I was so panicked yesterday when T.J. came up to me in the parking lot, I had to do something." I shook my head at the memory. "I just don't want to spend the rest of senior year scared."

Kerri slowed her steps. "Uh-oh," she muttered.

My eyes immediately scanned the hallway. Coming straight toward us were T.J. and some of his crew. As usual, guys were stopping to talk to them and girls were flirting with them, treating them like they ruled the school.

"Just keep walking," Kerri said under her breath.

Easy for her to say. My knees felt like jelly and my hands were shaking. I pretended to look at the math book I was carrying. Which is why I didn't see T.J. until he was right in my face.

"Thanks for the ride yesterday," he said, grinning. "You came along at just the right time."

I blinked. "But I—"

"You look really hot today," he continued. "Nice sweater."

Self-consciously I pulled my books to my chest. I was wearing a soft lavender cashmere sweater that fit pretty close.

Kerri glared at him. "What Maya looks like is none of your business. And she wouldn't give you a ride if you begged her, and you know it."

His friends smirked. "T.J.'s not the one doing the

begging," Jimmy Wright said.

"Maybe I'll drop by your house after school, Maya," T.J. called out as Kerri took my arm and marched me down the hall.

"Why is he doing this to me?" I asked, holding back a sob. "Why can't he leave me alone?"

"Because he's a jerk," Kerri replied angrily, her eyes blazing. "Maya, I think you ought to report the assault to the police. I hate that he's getting away with it!"

I blinked back tears. "I can't, Kerri. I just can't." We came to the corridor where we parted ways. Clutching my books to my chest, I walked blindly down the hall, struggling not to cry. How was I ever going to make it through my senior year?

"Come on, you guys! Look sharp!" Hannah Doyko, captain of the field hockey team and one of South Central's best players, was trying to get us revved at practice. "Think of how bad you want to beat Frontier!" Frontier was our big rival from last year. We'd be facing off against them again next week.

For the past fifteen minutes we'd been running drills up and down the field. I was tired and sweaty, and all I wanted was to collapse on the bench and guzzle my bottled water. At last Coach Dobson blew her whistle.

"Take a quick break," she ordered. "Then we'll scrimmage."

I ran to the bench, dropped my hockey stick, and grabbed my water bottle. I glanced at some guys hovering near the bench. Then I gasped. One of them was T.J.

"Hey, Maya," he said. "We just stopped by to watch a little hockey practice. I love those little skirts you hockey players wear."

The other guys started laughing. I turned away from them, fuming.

Coach Dobson blew her whistle again. "Scrimmage!" she shouted.

Without looking at the boys, I picked up my hockey stick and ran out on the field.

"I'll be watching!" T.J. called out. His friends laughed again.

*I hate him,* I thought angrily. Knowing T.J. was watching made it hard for me to concentrate.

*Come on, Maya,* I told myself, dribbling the ball down the pitch. *Keep your focus tight.* Our goalie, Ari Wiley, was ready to block me.

I waited until I was positioned within the circle, trying to channel all the anger and frustration I'd felt these past few weeks into my hockey stick. Suddenly I imagined T.J.'s smirking face on the ball. *Whack!* I struck it hard, sending it sailing cleanly into the goal cage.

"Whoa!" Ari exclaimed, her jaw dropping. She hadn't missed a block yet.

I shot her a grin.

"Maya, you rule!" Hannah shouted, jogging over.

For the first time in ages, I felt some of the stress fade away. I glanced over to the sidelines, but T.J. and his friends were gone.

I was exhausted when I walked into the castle at a little before five. I ached all over. All I wanted was a long, hot bath.

Peter and a bunch of other campaign people had set up camp in the study and in our dining room, and I was sure they'd infiltrated the living room too. CNN blared from the TV, cell phones were ringing, and I could hear the whir of the fax machine as it spit out paper.

So far, no sign of Marlene. Maybe I could make it to the bathtub before she got her claws into me.

"Where's my dad?" I asked as Peter gave me a hurried wave.

He tilted his head toward the study. "On the phone. Getting ready for the press conference," he explained.

"What else?" I joked, deciding to make a hasty retreat to my room. I'd almost made it to the stairs when a hand clamped down on my shoulder.

"Maya." Marlene smiled.

"Uh, hi, Marlene. I was just going to my room."

She held up a well-manicured finger. "Before you do, there's someone I'd like you to meet."

I shrugged. "Well, okay."

We walked into the living room. A man in black pants and a black turtleneck sat on our couch, flipping through a stack of magazines. A framed picture of me sat on the coffee table next to him instead of in its usual place on my dad's desk.

"Jack, this is Maya, Spencer's daughter," Marlene said. "Maya, this is Jack Paraud, owner of La Gamine salon. Jack has been retained as an image consultant for your father's campaign."

"Oh. Well, nice to meet you," I said, smiling slightly. I turned to go.

Marlene held my arm. "Wait, Maya. Jack is also here to help you."

"Me?" I repeated, staring at her.

She clucked her tongue. "As I said the other day, Maya. You can't waltz around town looking like . . . like . . ."

"A mess," Jack finished, but in a nice way. He gave me an apologetic hands-up gesture.

Marlene nodded. "We've been discussing some modifications to your look," she told me.

Jack stood up and stepped toward me. "Would you be willing to cut this?" he asked me, picking up a hunk of my hair and letting it drop. "Say a more sophisticated, shorter cut?"

"I . . . I don't think so," I stammered, caught off guard. I hadn't realized how far Marlene would take this makeover stuff. She really did want me to change my look—completely.

Just then my dad walked in. "Spencer," Marlene said, walking over to him. "We were just beginning Maya's makeover."

"You mean there's more?" I asked.

"Well, besides your hair and wardrobe, we need to groom you for the press," Marlene said, as if this was obvious. "You're going to need to know what questions will be thrown at you and how to answer them. Being a candidate's daughter isn't something you just wake up and do. It's going to take practice."

"Dad, do I have to do this?" I asked.

He ran his fingers through his hair. "It's up to you, Maya."

"But, Dad," I said. "Do you *want* me to do this?"

"Honey, it's up to you. I don't want to force you to do anything you don't want to do."

I could tell Marlene wasn't too crazy about his answer, but she kept it to herself. She was smart enough to know that her feedback wasn't wanted.

I looked from my dad to Jack to Marlene. I did want to make my dad happy, and I had a feeling that he wanted me to do it. And I didn't want to look like a fool during a press interview. I *could* use some tips. Plus, if I went along with their program, I might actually end up spending more time with my father. Maybe we would grow closer again.

"Well . . . okay," I said slowly, looking at my dad. "But only a trim to start."

Jack's lips curled into a smile. "My scissors will be gentle."

Marlene flipped open her date book. "Perfect. I'll schedule a session with a personal shopper at Nordstrom next week."

Marlene and Jack began to discuss their plans to make me over. I stood helplessly between them, feeling more insecure than ever. One new and improved Maya, coming right up. I just hope she turned out to be a lot happier than the present one.

"Please, Maya, come in," Valerie Sheridan said, motioning me inside her office on Tuesday afternoon. The room was bright and comfortable, furnished with a glass-topped desk, two upholstered chairs, and a matching sofa. Three framed prints of flowers hung on the muted pink walls. Dr. Sheridan was around thirty. She wore gray pants and a white cotton shirt, and she had short wavy blond hair.

She sat in one of the chairs in front of her desk, so I sat down in the other. I wasn't sure what to do.

"When you called me the other day, you said you had a lot on your mind," Dr. Sheridan started off.

I nodded.

"Well, I'm your sounding board. Where do you want to start?" she asked, smiling.

I looked down at my hands. Maybe this was a bad idea, I thought. Now that I was here, the idea of actually talking to a therapist seemed incredibly scary.

"Maya?" Dr. Sheridan prompted.

I licked my lips. "I . . . I . . . This is really hard for me," I said finally. "I've never done this before."

"We can go at your speed," she told me, smoothing back her hair. "No pressure."

She did seem nice. I took a breath. "I really miss my mom."

"Where is she?" Dr. Sheridan asked.

I swallowed the lump that always formed in my throat when I spoke of her. "She died almost two years ago." I sat there, not sure what to say. "I still miss her a lot," I added finally.

"Maya, that's completely understandable," Dr. Sheridan said.

"I know it's been a long time and I should be over

it, but it's so hard," I said. "I wish that I could just see her one more time. I wouldn't even care if she couldn't talk—like if she was lying in her bed, sick. If I could just feel her hand once more," I whispered, the lump growing bigger.

Dr. Sheridan nodded. "Of course you wish you could see her again."

"I even dream about her sometimes," I admitted. "In my dreams I tell her everything about my life, and she listens and tells me what to do." I smiled sadly. "But in the morning I can't remember her advice."

Dr. Sheridan listened patiently to everything I said, and when I started crying a little, she didn't tell me to stop, just handed me a tissue and asked if I wanted some water.

"What about your dad, Maya? How is your relationship with him?" she asked a few minutes later, taking some notes.

I sniffled. "He's always been overprotective of me and really into his career. But lately he's become more of both." I thought about how he wouldn't talk about Mom. "And he never wants to talk about anything important."

"Such as. . . ?" the doctor prompted.

"My mom. Me. How I feel," I said, realizing how mad I felt about that. "I try to talk to him about stuff, but he never seems to have time for me. And he's almost always surrounded by a team of people. So I never get to really say what I want." I shrugged miserably.

Dr. Sheridan nodded again. "How does that make you feel?"

"Sad," I said quietly. Then I told her how Marlene was trying to make me over, and how I'd agreed to let her. "I want to do the right thing for my dad," I said. "But I don't think I can compete with his work for his attention."

She asked me some more questions about home, and the more I talked, the easier it got.

"You mentioned a boy on your message?" Dr. Sheridan asked then.

I felt my cheeks flush. When I called her from my car, I'd been so shaken up about running into T.J. that I'd blurted out things that I would never have been able to say in person. "Well . . ."

"Is this an ex-boyfriend?" she asked.

"*No.*" I told her how I'd had a crush on T.J. and how I'd kind of pursued him. "But then—but then there was this party, and . . ." I picked at my cuticles. "He, um, he . . . forced himself on me," I whispered.

"What do you mean, *forced*?" she asked gently.

"Well, he . . . he kept kissing me even after I told him to stop. And he . . . he . . ." I started to cry. "He wouldn't stop touching me. He ripped my shirt, and

I thought he was going to . . . going to rape me."

Dr. Sheridan took my hand. "But he didn't?"

"No," I said, choking back a sob. "He threw me down on the couch, but . . . I was able to get away."

"Did you call the police?"

"No." I wiped my tears away. "I haven't told anybody except for my best friends. T.J. was the first boy I ever kissed. I mean, how do you make a guy stop if he doesn't listen to 'no'? And I can't figure out if it was because of something *I* did."

Dr. Sheridan sighed. "The problem isn't with you. It's with T.J." She put down her notepad. "This is a lot to deal with on your own. A good first step would be to have an open dialogue with your dad. Maybe then you'll be able to talk to him about the things that are bothering you, like Marlene and his campaign." She leaned back in her chair. "Maybe you'll even be able to tell him about T.J."

I shook my head. My dad didn't even want me to date. If he knew how far out of hand things had gotten with T.J., well, he'd be more overprotective than ever. And he'd be really angry with me for disobeying him. "There's no way."

She didn't comment on that. "For now, I'd like you to keep a journal. Write down what you'd like to tell your mom, dad, and T.J. Sometimes seeing things in print makes them easier to say." Then she smiled at me. "I think that's enough for today. Let's talk again next week."

On the way home I stopped at Bella's Stationery Shop, where I bought a blank book with gold stars and moons on the cover. That would be my journal.

Three hours later I threw myself back on my bed, staring at my collection of antique dolls, allowing the thumping bass of NAS to numb my brain. Ever since dinner I'd been trying to write in my new journal. All I'd managed so far was a goofy caricature of Mr. Anderson, my physics teacher, and some pretty way-out sketches of prom dresses. I knew what I wanted to say, but somehow it just wouldn't come through my pen and onto the paper.

*Keeping a diary is silly,* I thought. *If I have something to say to Dad, I should just say it. Why write it down?*

But I knew I couldn't tell Dad what was on my mind. I didn't have the courage. *Besides, Jessica is the writer, not me,* I thought, irritated, tossing my pen across the room just as my dad opened my door and stuck his head inside.

"Dad!" I exclaimed as the pen narrowly missed his head. He eyed the stereo, the pen, and then me.

"Everything okay?" he asked uncertainly.

The sight of him, slightly rumpled in his khakis

and sweater, suddenly made me crumble. We'd been so close before my mom's death, and I missed that. I missed *him*. A lot.

"Maya?" my father said, looking at me with real concern. "Are you all right?"

I took a deep breath, praying that he really did want to know what was going on in my life.

Because I was about to tell him.

# Chapter 5

**I**f you really want to know the truth, Dad, I'm not okay." I cleared my throat. "I haven't been for a while." It had been a long time since I'd been honest with my father. "And it's not helping that you're never around," I added, my voice catching.

He came over and sat down on my bed. "Maya," he said, his voice full of worry. "What's got you so upset?"

"My life," I croaked out, not sure what to talk about first.

I decided to start with the easy stuff. "Every time I walk into this house, someone tells me how to sit or what to say or what to wear. I can't even go into the kitchen without Marlene thrusting a newspaper in my face or telling me I'm a mess. I'm sick of it, Dad." My hands were shaking.

"But Maya, you know that this won't last forever. If I'm going to win the campaign—"

"I don't care about the campaign!" I burst out. "Ever since Mom died we haven't been able to talk. You've thrown yourself into your work. Things have been really hard for me this year, and just when I think they can't get any worse, you announce that you're running for office, and now things *are* worse!"

My dad held up his hands. "Whoa! Maya, yelling isn't going to get us anywhere. If you calm down, maybe we can discuss how you're feeling like rational adults."

I swallowed. "But Dad, I'm not an adult. I'm sixteen. I mean . . . I need you," I said, wanting to spill it all. "I need you around, not always running off to some fund-raiser or holed up in your office doing research, or surrounded by a dozen people. I know that this is important to you, and I'm trying to help out, but . . ."

I looked away, my eyes falling on the framed photograph of my mom, dad, and me that sits on my dresser. It was taken on my tenth birthday. I looked like a goober, with short goofy hair and toothpicks for legs, but my mom looked as pretty as ever, her hair, still thick, long and wavy, pulled back in a ponytail, her smile wide, her brown eyes bright. My dad's arms were around us both, hugging us, pulling us close.

A tear slid down my cheek. "I miss you," I

45

whispered. "I miss having someone I can talk to about stuff."

"Maya." He reached over and put his hand on my arm. "I'm still your dad. That hasn't changed. How can you ever, *ever* think that anything would come before you?"

I laughed hollowly through my tears. "Because I feel like you don't have time for me." I rubbed my sleeve across my face. "I mean, we never get to talk. We don't really know each other anymore. I just want my old dad back," I told him, sniffling. "What's so great about being a successful attorney or becoming lieutenant governor of Wisconsin if you never have any time to spend with your family?" I bit my lip. "What's left of it, anyway."

Suddenly my father's handsome face seemed tired. The eyes that were always so bright looked defeated, and the hands that were always writing, directing, moving in a thousand different directions, lay limp in his lap.

"And I have to tell you something else," I said. "I called that therapist. I went to see her, Dad. I had to. I need someone to listen to my problems. I know you don't think it's the right thing to do, but . . ." I gazed at my father, waiting for him to get angry.

He didn't. Instead he just touched my hair. "You're right," he said finally, after a long, labored sigh. "You're right, Maya."

"I am?"

"Ask anyone on my staff what my top priority is, and they'll say it's you. Because that's what I always say. But actions speak louder than words, and although in my heart I put you first, in my daily life I haven't. And I'm sorry."

I couldn't believe he'd said that.

"I've been so wrapped up in the campaign that I haven't been able to focus on anything else," he confessed. "I want you to come to me with your problems, honey. I want to be there for you." His voice cracked. "I don't blame you if you don't believe me, but I want to be a part of your life, Maya."

Fresh tears welled up as he pulled me toward him. "I care about you more than anything on this earth, Maya. I—"

I didn't wait to hear more before hugging him back as hard he was hugging me. "I love you too, Daddy." All the hurt and pain of the last few weeks seemed to slip away in that one powerful embrace. Just having my father back again, knowing that he was there for me, meant everything.

"I'm so sorry your mom can't be here for you," he said. "But I can. Let's make a pact, Maya. An honesty pact. I'll be one hundred percent here for you. One hundred percent straight with you. If you'll be the same with me."

"Okay, Dad." What else could I say? I wished I could be honest with him. I wished I could tell him everything.

But how could I? If he knew about T.J., would he ever think of me the same way again?

# Chapter 6

**I** had chickened out that night. Telling my dad about T.J. would have embarrassed me beyond belief. *No matter what anyone says,* I thought, *there's some stuff that parents should never know about. It's just better that way.*

The next morning my dad was scanning the *Madison Herald,* drinking what was probably his third cup of coffee, and checking who knew what on his laptop as usual. When I walked into the kitchen and took out the Raisin Bran, he looked up from the screen.

"Good morning, honey. You look nice."

"You think?" I was wearing a faded pair of jeans and a long-sleeved navy T-shirt with this funky beaded choker Erin had loaned me. For the first time in a while, I'd actually taken some care in getting dressed.

My dad spread some jam on his toast. Then he looked at me, his eyes serious. "I meant what I said last night, Maya. I'm really glad you told me how you felt. Remember our pact—from now on we're completely honest with each other. Right?"

I picked up my orange juice glass and clinked it against his coffee mug. "Deal."

My dad laughed as he thumbed through a stack of papers, eventually pulling out a letter-sized envelope and handing it to me. "The other day I dropped by the WDGY radio station, and they gave me these. Apparently they thought it'd be funny to have me boogying at a rock concert. Interested in going with one of your girlfriends?"

I opened the envelope and my eyes widened. "They gave you Oneida tickets?" Oneida was the hottest college band around—and one of my favorites! In fact they had this great, depressing song, "Who Never Was," which was in permanent rotation on my stereo.

"Thanks!" I couldn't wait to tell my friends. They were all huge Oneida fans. I fingered the two tickets. Who would I ask?

As I was trying to decide, Marlene came in from the dining room. "Maya, I'm glad you're still here. I wrote up some mock interview questions that I wanted to go over with you."

"Now?" I asked, looking at the clock. "I have to get to school."

She waved her hand. "This won't take long." She motioned for me to follow her into the living room. We sat down on opposite ends of the couch.

"All right. Pretend I'm a member of the press," she began.

"Okay," I said, feeling a bit nervous.

"What do you think about your father running for lieutenant governor?" she asked, her eyes boring into me.

"I think it's great," I said honestly.

Marlene smiled.

"But I keep wondering if we'll have even less time to spend together," I continued.

She frowned. "Don't be too honest, Maya. You didn't need to add that second part."

"Oh," I said, biting my lip.

"All right. What do you think your father will bring to this position?"

I smiled. "He's a total workaholic. I know he'll work really, really hard for the people of Wisconsin."

Marlene frowned again. "Maya, try to avoid such negativity. Instead of saying he's a workaholic, why not focus on how dedicated he is to his profession?"

I hunched my shoulders. I knew I wasn't going to be any good at this.

She asked me a few more questions, and I tried

hard to say what I thought she wanted.

Marlene loved it.

"We'll get there," she said as I gathered my books. I slipped them into my backpack and headed out to my car.

I slid in behind the wheel and started the BMW. As it warmed up I took my journal out of my bag. I smoothed back a fresh, creamy white page and began to write.

One hundred percent honest. That's what I'm supposed to be, right? So how come I feel like such a liar? Every time I told Marlene how I really felt during this "mock interview" thing, she said that was the wrong answer. And every time I said something that seemed like a lie, she thought it sounded perfect.

You know what? I don't even think I know what honesty is.

Kerri was my first choice for the concert. She loves Oneida even more than I do.

"A week from Friday?" she echoed after I showed her the tickets at school that morning. "That's the South Central–Lakeland game," she wailed. "I can't believe it!"

"There's no way you can bail?" I asked.

"Not if I want to stay on the cheerleading squad."

Kerri sighed. "Guess you'll have to ask somebody else."

Ha, easier said than done. I couldn't make up my mind whether to ask Jessica or Erin, so I decided I'd ask whomever I saw first. And that ended up being Jess, outside math class.

"Oh, Maya, I'd love to . . . but I can't. My cousin Nicole's engagement party is that night. There's a big surprise dinner and everything. My aunt has been planning it for over a month."

"Oh," I said. I hadn't expected another rejection.

"Sorry," Jessica said. "Maybe another time."

I waved halfheartedly as she went into her classroom. Who would have thought it'd be so hard to find takers for Oneida tickets?

Just then Erin rounded the corner. In her magenta shirt and sparkly platform sneakers she was hard to miss. I dashed toward her. "Erin, are you free a week from Friday night?" I blurted out.

She shook her two braids. "I have to work on the set for the school play every night for the next two weeks, remember?"

"Oh. Right." She had told me about it at Bernie's, but I'd forgotten.

Kerri joined us. "So who's the lucky girl?" she asked.

I sighed. "No one. You guys all turned me down."

Kerri leaned closer to me. "You could always ask Luke, you know."

"I told you—I don't want to go out with anyone. Besides, we'd be alone in a car." I couldn't help shuddering. "It's way too risky."

"It doesn't have to be risky," Erin said. "Why not see if you can meet him at the concert? That way you'll be perfectly safe."

"That's not a bad idea," Kerri agreed. "Maybe you should give it a try."

I hesitated. "Well . . . won't that sound weird, though? Asking him to meet me there?"

Kerri shook her head. "Absolutely not."

"Luke!" Erin called.

"Erin, no!" I whispered, but Erin was already waving at someone—obviously Luke—who was behind me.

I could barely bring myself to turn around. But sure enough, Luke Perez was headed our way. He did look cute. *But so did T.J.*, I remembered. *And look where that got me.*

"Hey, Luke, did you get that physics homework done?" Erin asked him.

I pretended to be very busy looking for something in my notebook. I couldn't believe she was doing this.

"I'm not taking physics," Luke said, his dark eyes

glancing from Erin to me to Kerri. I wanted to die right then.

"Oops! I thought you were in my class," Erin told him, then poked me in the ribs. "Anyway, guess what Maya's got?"

He shrugged.

I blushed. "Um, Oneida tickets. They're playing a week from Friday," I said, wanting to strangle Erin for using such a lame line to lure him over.

"You scored Oneida tickets?" Luke said, his eyebrows shooting up. "I love that band!"

"My dad got the tickets for free," I explained, my face warm.

"Maya will only go with someone who likes them as much as she does," Kerri chimed in. "If she can't find anybody, she's going to stay home."

"We'll catch you in chorus, Maya," Erin said, squeezing my arm.

Kerri waved. "Bye, Luke."

Luke offered me a smile after they had gone. "Your friends seem nice."

"Yeah," I said.

We stood there for what felt like eternity. I was convinced that Luke could hear my heart pounding— that's how nervous I was. I'd always been timid and nervous around guys. But now I was beyond nervous. I was straight-out scared.

I took a deep breath. *Keep cool, Maya,* I told myself. *Nothing bad is going to happen to you in the middle of South Central.*

"So," Luke said finally.

"So," I said back, scuffing my shoe on the floor. There was no way I was going to be able to ask him out.

"If you want someone to go with, I'll go," Luke said, giving me a crooked smile.

I blinked. "I . . . I . . ."

Why was Luke *really* interested in me? Was it because he'd heard some of the things T.J.'s friends had been saying about me? Did he think I was easy or something?

Luke must have sensed I was having second thoughts. "Or if you don't want me to, that's okay too," he said, sounding a little awkward.

I closed my eyes for a moment. Could I trust him? "Can I meet you there?" I asked, feeling kind of dumb.

He shrugged. "Sure. That's cool."

"Okay, then . . . let's go together." I managed to smile. "Um, well, I guess I'll see you there, then."

"Okay." He smiled, then turned and melted away in the crowd.

*Luke isn't T.J. There's nothing to be frightened of,* I told myself as I walked down the hall to my next class.

But I didn't really believe it.

# *Chapter 7*

**K**erri's eyes widened. "You did it?"

Erin clapped her hands. "I'm so proud of you!"

"Me too," Jessica said as the three of them clustered around me in the noisy chorus room. I'd just given them an instant replay of my conversation with Luke. "You guys are going to make such a cute couple!"

"It's kind of early for that," I said, feeling nervous. "I mean, it's just one date."

"Okay, people," Mr. Calvert, our chorus teacher, motioned for us to get into our places on the risers. "Spit out the gum, Charlie," he told Charlie Simpson, a junior, while motioning for the accompanist to set up. "Can't sing 'Amazing Grace' and blow bubbles at the same time."

We shuffled into our spots—Erin and I were both sopranos, Jessica and Kerri, altos. Mr. Calvert began leading us through our warm-up vocals before moving on to the hymn.

All through grade school and junior high, I'd kind of avoided singing. My voice wasn't that great, and I was always terrified I'd have to do a solo in front of everybody or something. But Jessica had convinced me that chorus would be fun, and over the past few years I'd decided she was right.

It felt good to sing, to know that my voice was part of those soaring harmonies. Besides, chorus was the only class Kerri, Jessica, Erin, and I had together. It had become one of my favorite periods.

*Or at least it used to be*, I thought resentfully, catching sight of T.J. Miller for the first time that day. He stood in the tenor section on the far side of the risers, one row below me, his head tilted to the side. The way the risers curved he ended up facing me slightly, and it was hard not to look at him.

He glanced up at me. Before I had a chance to look away, he winked.

My stomach clenched. What was I thinking, agreeing to go out with Luke like that? I could feel my chest tightening. The more I thought about Luke, the more I started to panic. What if he turned out to be like T.J.? Or what if he was only interested in me because of the disgusting rumors T.J. had started? Maybe saying yes to Luke was a bad move.

A really bad move. Maybe I'd better tell him I'd changed my mind.

Six days later, on Tuesday afternoon, I still hadn't broken my date with Luke. Kerri was gabbing about the latest cheer squad squabble to Jessica and Erin when I dropped into the empty seat they'd saved for me at lunch. I tried to look interested as I took out my chicken-salad-stuffed pita and Snapple. But I was still thinking about breaking the date.

Suddenly Kerri's fingers waved in front of my face. "Is anyone home?"

I blushed. "Sorry. Just spacing, I guess."

"Erin was just telling us about this guy in her study hall," Jessica said, popping a pretzel into her mouth.

Erin rolled her eyes. "It's nothing, really. He sits behind me in study hall, and has been kind of flirting with me since school started." Erin smiled, then shrugged. "And he's kind of cute."

Kerri took a sip of her water. "So what's the problem?"

Erin sighed. "I just don't feel like getting to know another guy. I only want Keith."

"But Erin, he's so far away," Jessica reminded her as Matt Fowler came over.

"Howdy," he said, dropping into a seat and

giving Kerri a kiss. We all smiled at him. But secretly I was disappointed that he'd joined us. Nothing against Matt, but I liked it better when it was just us girls.

"Anything good?" Kerri asked Matt, peering at his tray. "Is that stew *supposed* to look like vomit?"

He arched his eyebrows. "Kerri, I was trying not to notice that."

I bit into my pita as the two of them began whispering and laughing together. *How does Kerri do it?* I wondered. How did she manage to act so relaxed around guys?

"I know Keith is far away!" Erin told Jessica. "Especially since he hasn't e-mailed me for three days now. Maybe we're losing our spark," she added unhappily.

"So maybe you should flirt with the guy in study hall," Jess suggested.

"Maybe," Erin agreed. "I guess it couldn't hurt."

Jessica leaned across the table. "So who do you guys think is going to win the game on Friday?" she asked us.

"My money's on the Chiefs," Erin said with a smile.

"Hey!" Kerri squealed, bumping into my shoulder. "That tickles!" Matt had his arms around her waist, his hands on her stomach.

"Oh, it does, does it?" Matt asked, burying his face in her neck.

Erin rolled her eyes. "Ah, young love."

"Matt, no!" Kerri protested, laughing.

Jessica had started talking about the yearbook, but I was having a hard time paying attention with Kerri dodging Matt beside me. This didn't really seem like the right place to carry on like that.

"I never realized you were so ticklish," Matt said, tickling Kerri in the ribs.

"Well, I am," Kerri told him, trying to wriggle out of his grasp. "So quit it!"

"There's no stopping the Tickler," Matt said, his hands all over her.

Kerri's face was flushed. "No, Matt. Stop!" she managed to gasp.

But Matt didn't stop.

And I was starting to get nervous. Kerri obviously wasn't enjoying this anymore. *Why don't boys get it?* I wondered angrily. *No is supposed to mean no!* I glanced at Matt who wasn't listening to Kerri's pleas. Was every guy like T.J.?

"Matt! Cut it out!" Kerri squealed again as her face turned red. Tears started forming in her eyes.

*No means no . . . no means no . . .* The words ran across my mind like an electronic sign. I couldn't take it any longer. "Hey!" I yelled. I stood up and pushed Matt roughly on the shoulder. "Didn't you hear her say no? Leave her alone!"

Instantly Matt let go of Kerri. Her arm fell to the table, hitting my bottle of Snapple and sending it splashing onto the floor.

The cafeteria went silent.

"I was just fooling around, Maya," Matt said quietly.

I swallowed. Everyone in the cafeteria was staring at us.

"Yeah, we were just playing," Kerri said, her voice concerned.

"I . . . I . . ." My face grew hot with embarrassment as I looked at my friends' pitying faces. And I knew that the whole cafeteria was probably staring at me. Grabbing my books, I ran for the door.

"Maya! Maya, wait," Kerri called after me.

But I didn't stop. I was dying of humiliation. Kerri and Matt had just been kidding around. Why did I do that? There was no way I could pretend that I was normal and that everything was okay.

And this proved it.

I wasn't like my friends.

I wasn't like anybody.

# Chapter 8

"**I** can't go," I repeated, shaking my head. "I can't!"

"Maya, if you don't want to go out with Luke, you don't have to," Dr. Sheridan said. We were in her office that afternoon after school. I'd told her what had happened in the cafeteria.

"I don't?" I whispered.

She shook her head. "Maya, the whole reason for a date is because two people like each other and want to spend time together. If you're not interested in Luke, then there's no point in going out with him."

I hunched my shoulders. "It's just that I don't feel ready for all that stuff. Like when Kerri told Matt to stop and he didn't . . . it just freaked me out." My voice was shaky. "It made me feel like the scene with T.J. was happening again."

Dr. Sheridan took a sip of her coffee. "From what you just described, it sounds like Kerri's no was said in jest, as part of the 'I like you' game. The no you said to T.J. was completely different. But there's no need to be ashamed of reacting the way you did. You've been through a lot, Maya. That's why you misinterpreted them."

"But if I got the signals so wrong with Kerri and Matt, how can I trust myself to get them right when it comes to me?" I wailed. "What do you think I should do?"

No matter how upset I got, Dr. Sheridan always kept her voice at a soothing, even pitch. "Maya, I'm not here to tell you what choices to make. I do think that if you met Luke at the concert, you could have a nice time. You'd be in a crowded place, doing something you genuinely want to be doing. It sounds like the perfect date for you."

I stared at my knees. "I'll think about it," I said finally.

"Are you sure this is my color?" I asked, squinting dubiously at my lilac-colored nails.

Erin capped the bottle of polish. "Trust me, dahling," she joked in a fake accent. "I know nails."

It was Wednesday evening, our monthly Girls' Night, when Erin, Jessica, Kerri, and I got together for gossip, junk food, and beauty treatments. We'd been hanging out in my room for the past hour, giving each other manicures, steaming our faces, and watching movies on cable.

A box of pizza, half eaten, sat open on top of my desk. Jessica picked up a slice and dangled it, dripping, over the box. "Too bad you have to wait for your nails to dry," she teased. She tilted her head back, opened her mouth, and made a big show of taking a long, chewy bite. Then she grinned and held the pizza for me so I could take a bite without ruining my manicure.

"Thanks, Jess," I said with my mouth full.

Kerri reached into her purse and took out a small white box. "Look what I got today," she said. She didn't sound pleased. She opened the box and held up a turquoise pendant set in silver, on a silver chain.

"It's beautiful!" I said.

"You think so?" She dropped the necklace back into the box and handed it to me. "Then *you* keep it. Because there's no way I'm wearing it."

"Why not?" Erin asked. "If Keith sent me something like that—"

"The necklace isn't from Matt," Kerri said. "It's from my ex-father. A birthday present."

"But your birthday was a month ago!" Jessica said.

Kerri rolled her eyes. "Exactly. Like this necklace

is supposed to make up for that and the seven birthdays he wasn't around for."

"Okay, he definitely blew it," I agreed. "But maybe he knows he messed up, and he's trying to show you he still cares."

"He's trying to buy me," Kerri snapped. She threw the box across the room, and the necklace fell out onto the floor.

I carefully picked up the necklace and put it back in its box.

"Sorry, Maya," Kerri said at once. "It's just that after being gone for seven years, he sends me e-mails that are filled with lies about where he's living. Which just goes to prove that he never really wanted to see me again, after all. And now he sends me this birthday present! Does he really think I'm going to be his daughter again, after all that?"

There was a long, awkward silence. I didn't know what to say. I couldn't understand why Kerri's father had acted the way he did. But then, sometimes I didn't understand my own dad either.

Erin deliberately changed the subject. "I got an e-mail from Keith today, finally," she told us. "It was pretty cute. He put a row of little dancing bananas at the top of the screen and underneath he wrote, 'Are you peeling as sad as I am that we're apart?'"

"I don't know how you can stand this long-distance thing," Jessica said. "You never get to see him! Don't you feel like you'll forget what he's really like? E-mail can only go so far."

"I could never do it," Kerri agreed.

Erin shrugged. "I wish he was here, but he's not—so what can I do? It's not so bad." She leaned back on the bed and closed her eyes. "You know, when I hear from Keith it's like my whole day is better. I feel like I'm walking around school with this secret, this fabulous guy that no one here knows about." She opened her eyes and propped herself up on her elbows. "But I miss the physical stuff."

I knew Erin hadn't slept with Keith, but apparently they'd come pretty close. I guessed once you went that far with someone, it was kind of hard to go back.

Jessica took a sip of her soda. "I ran into Alex today in the hall. He was wearing the sweater I got him last Christmas." A sad look flitted across her face. "I kind of miss him."

"You guys were together a long time," I said, feeling sad for her. She and Alex had once been almost inseparable.

"That's another good thing about a long-distance relationship," Erin said. "If we break up, I won't have to see him around school every five seconds."

"There are a lot of guys right here who would

love to be with you," Jessica reminded her. "Maybe you should give one of them a try."

"Those guys just want to go out with this year's homecoming queen." Erin shook her head. "This one guy asked me out today. . . ."

"Who?" we all asked in unison.

"Leif Bulova," she replied.

"Who?" Kerri asked, wrinkling her nose.

"The name sounds familiar," Jessica said. She snapped her fingers. "The waify vegan guy who looks like Beck?"

Erin nodded. "Yep. I walked by as he was handing out leaflets for an antileather demonstration happening at the university. Apparently he liked me because"—she paused dramatically—"I was the only homecoming queen candidate who didn't wear any animal products. You know, most of the girls had leather shoes."

"That's sweet, Erin," I said, smiling.

"Maybe you should go out with him," Kerri suggested. When Erin rolled her eyes, Kerri added, "Just for fun. It can't hurt to go on one date. Take your mind off Keith for a while."

Erin shook her head. "Leif's too weird." She turned to me. "Speaking of dates," she said, "I'm volunteering my services to be your personal shopper. You're going to need a totally killer outfit for that Oneida concert."

I picked at a piece of lint on the bedspread. "Thanks anyway, but . . . I'm not going."

"What?" Kerri shrieked.

Erin pleaded. "You have to go."

"You can't back out," Jessica said, her eyes intense. "You'll have a great time!"

I studied my nails, which were finally dry. "You know, I could get used to this lilac nail polish," I said.

"Maya!" Jessica grabbed my shoulders and shook me.

I sighed. "I'm scared, okay? I mean, Luke seems nice, but I don't really know him."

"But you'll never know *any* guy if you don't take a chance," Kerri said.

"Yeah, but I made such an idiot of myself in the cafeteria," I mumbled. "Luke probably thinks I'm a big geek anyway."

"He doesn't think you're a geek," Erin protested. "He really likes you. It's so obvious!"

"I don't know," I said.

Just then there was a knock on my door. It opened slightly, and my father poked his head in. "Hi, girls. Maya, do you have a copy of your field-hockey practice schedule?"

"Um, sure. Here," I said, walking over to my desk and taking it off my corkboard.

"Marlene is making some appointments for you, and I didn't want them to conflict with your schedule." He smiled at my friends. "So which lucky girl is going to see Oneida?"

For a moment, the honesty pact flew into my mind. But I couldn't tell him about Luke—I wasn't allowed to go out on dates. And I was planning to break the date anyway. So I said, "Kerri's going, Dad."

Kerri looked at me and then at my dad, and smiled. "Yeah, Mr. Greer. I can't wait."

"Well, have fun. Night, Maya." He shut the door.

Kerri scowled at me. "Why are you lying to your father about who you're going with?" she demanded.

"Are you kidding?" I asked. "My dad would never let me go to a concert with a boy! He doesn't want me to date till I'm a senior in *college*." And maybe that wasn't a bad idea.

"Maya, you just went to all the trouble of lying to your father about who you're going to the concert with," Jessica said. "So you might as well go through with it and go with Luke." Jessica had a knack for making things sound logical—even when they weren't.

Erin jumped up off the bed. "And let us take you shopping!"

Kerri squeezed my arm. "You can page me from the concert as many times as you want and I'll call you back," she said. "Date support."

I knew they all wanted what was best for me. And lately, I didn't seem to know what that was, so how could I not listen to them?

"Okay, I'll go," I said finally. "But just to the concert. And I'm meeting him there. That's it."

Kerri and Jessica whooped.

Erin pointed to my wallet on my desk and grinned. "Get ready, Maya. Because we've got some serious shopping to do before Friday night."

Wednesday night

Another Girls' Night. Tonight was fun. But now that everyone's gone home, it's so quiet here. I wish I had a sister. It would be like having a friend who's always around, who never has to go home at the end of the evening.

Erin painted my nails lilac. I wasn't sure about it at first, but now I like it.

Friday night is the Oneida concert. I wonder how it will go. Funny, I don't remember ever seeing Luke with another girl at South Central. He's so cute, I can't believe he hasn't had a zillion girlfriends. I hope he's really as nice as he seems. I mean, I can see for myself that he's nice at school, but I wouldn't say I've had the best judgment lately.

I wish Mom could be here to see me, to give me some

advice. This concert will be my first real date. It's kind of embarrassing. I mean, here I am, 16, and I've only kissed two people: Mike Scott, back when I was in eighth grade and I got stuck playing spin the bottle at Kerri's house (I would hardly label that a kiss), and T.J. Wow, some experience, huh?

MOM, I REALLY NEED YOU.

I miss her so much. My friends are great, but there's no one like your mom to help you pick out your clothes, or tell you what your hair looks like and stuff. The thing is, you don't realize that until you don't have a mom anymore. If I told Kerri and Erin and Jess that, they'd feel bad for me, but they wouldn't really get it. Sometimes it's hard to be around them and have to pretend that I'm not sad about my mom. It's like I have to fake being happy, like I'm always on, even with my closest friends. I don't know what else to do. It would be a drag being around someone who's still mourning her mother almost two years after she died.

But I am mourning her. I can't help it. Dr. Sheridan told me that's perfectly normal, but I don't care. It still hurts. When I think of all the things Mom missed out on doing—making full professor at the college, taking that sabbatical in Rome she always talked about, watching me grow up, growing old with Dad ... it makes me so sad I think I could curl up and die.

Sometimes I don't know how I can go on without her.

# Chapter 9

"**W**hat about this?" Erin held up a short, sequined aqua miniskirt. "This says *rock star*."

"Yeah, and it says a few other things too," I said, shaking my head. "I don't want to give Luke the wrong impression."

She fingered the fabric. "Maybe *I'll* try this on."

It was Thursday afternoon, and Erin, Jessica, and I had been at the Millwood Mall for about two hours, and already my arms were killing me from all the bags we held. Erin was like a fashion commando, darting in and out of stores, dragging me from one end of the colonnade to the other. She knew this place like the back of her henna-tattooed hand.

It was fun, though. Money was no object; my dad was always cool with whatever I spent, although I did rein Erin in when she tried to talk me into a $250 bag. Her philosophy was that I had to have at least three outfits to choose from. And when Erin said "outfit," she meant from head to toe. "Accessorize" was her middle name.

"Too bad Kerri had to work today," Jessica said as we waited for Erin to return from the dressing room. "We could have used her help carrying all this stuff."

After Erin decided to pass on the sequined miniskirt, we left the store, heading back into the throng of shoppers in the mall. "You didn't finish telling us about your date," I said to Erin. After a lot of prodding from Jessica, Erin had actually agreed to go out with Leif Bulova.

"Ugh," Erin groaned. "Do I have to? I'd like to erase it from my memory forever."

"Yes, you have to!" Jessica insisted.

Erin sighed. "Okay, so we go to the Cellar after school. We decided to split a small mushroom pizza—no meat, of course. The pizza comes, and Leif says, 'Before we eat, I've got to give thanks to the gods.'"

Jessica and I laughed as Erin imitated Leif's high, wispy voice.

"So I'm like, okay, whatever," Erin continued. "I think he's just going to bow his head and meditate or something. But no." She paused dramatically.

"What did he do?" I asked.

"He stood up right in the middle of the Cellar—

which was packed, by the way—and started, I don't know . . . *shimmying.*"

"What?" Jessica said.

"He closed his eyes and made these weird yelping sounds," Erin said. "And he was dancing around like this." Erin held her arms up over her head and shook her whole body, hopping up and down and yelling, "Whoop! Yeep! Yawp!"

"Oh, my god," I gasped.

Jessica started laughing.

Erin stopped dancing. "Everybody was staring at us. I wanted to hide under the table. I would have if it wasn't so greasy under there."

"What did he think he was doing?" Jessica asked.

"Well, when he finally stopped making an idiot of himself, he sat down and told me it was his own religion. He made it up. And that's how you say grace in the Church of Leif."

I was laughing so hard I had to stop and put down my bags. "Oh, my god," I repeated. "What did you do?"

"I told him that the Church of Erin forbids me to date members of the Church of Leif, and I ran for it. I've been blowing off his phone calls ever since." She turned to Jessica and added, "I'd like to remind you this was all *your* idea."

"I'm sorry, Erin," Jessica said, still laughing. "I

didn't realize he was such a freak."

All of a sudden Erin's mouth dropped. "Oh, great." Before I could react, she yanked us into a shoe store, darting behind a boot display.

"What's wrong?" Jessica asked.

"It's him," Erin said, peeking out into the mall. "He's here!"

I looked out of the corner of my eye. "He's coming, Erin."

"Terrific!" She grabbed a boot and pretended to be checking out the price.

"Erin? Erin, that *is* you," a soft male voice said. Leif walked into the store, his wispy hair tucked behind his ears, his gaze fixed on Erin's face. He had a canvas satchel slung over his back and a bag of organic potato chips in his hand.

"Oh, hi, Leif. These are my friends, Jessica and Maya," Erin said.

But Leif wasn't listening. He was staring around at his surroundings, noticing for the first time where he was. Then he looked at Erin with horror.

"What are you doing?" he practically shrieked, ripping the boot from her hands. Potato chips dropped on the carpet. "That's not imitation, you know."

"Get a grip," Erin said, yanking the boot back. "I like this. It has style."

"It's leather," Leif said tightly.

"Oh, good," Erin said, sounding relieved. "I hate that fake stuff."

Leif's lips pressed together in a frown. I knew Erin was trying to goad him, and I have to say I felt a little sorry for him. The guy was obviously very into his cause.

"I guess I misjudged you," Leif said, crossing his arms over his chest. "Don't bother calling me again."

"That guy is, like, seriously delusional," Erin remarked as he stalked out. She looked at Jessica and me and we all started to laugh.

"Can I help you?" The sales clerk, who looked about our age, smiled at us. He was very cute, slim with short brown hair, wearing jeans, a v-neck sweater, and biker boots.

"No thanks," Erin replied. "We were just hiding from somebody."

The clerk glanced down at our feet. "Your feet are so small," he said to Erin. "There's a beautiful pair of sandals over here that would look great on you." He led her away to look at the shoes.

Jess and I browsed around for a few minutes while the guy chatted with Erin. I could tell from the way her face was lighting up that she liked him, so it was no surprise that when we left, she revealed that she'd given him her e-mail address.

"You seemed to like him," I said as we headed toward Banana Republic.

She sniffed. "He's okay. But he's not Keith."

"Oh, my god," Jessica gasped. I could feel her body flinch.

"What?" I asked, a little scared.

"Look." She nodded toward a shop across the mall. Alex and Gretchen Jenkins, a pretty brunette junior, were standing in front of the CD store, looking at the display. Gretchen held a pretzel in her hand, and she was breaking off little pieces, feeding them to Alex. They were both laughing.

"I don't believe it," Erin said.

"Do you think. . . ?" Jessica began, her eyes welling with tears. She couldn't bring herself to finish the sentence.

"Maybe they're just friends," I said. But privately I didn't believe that. The way Gretchen was feeding the pretzel to Alex, the way he was touching her shoulder . . . they looked like a couple.

"I can't believe he would do this so soon," Erin said. "You guys just broke up!"

"Erin!" I scolded, slapping her on the arm. She could be so thoughtless sometimes.

Jessica shook her head. "I made the biggest mistake of my life, breaking up with him," she whispered.

I leaned close to her. "Don't torture yourself," I whispered. "You did what you felt was right."

Jessica nodded, but there was no getting rid of the miserable look in her dark eyes. "I know this sounds stupid, but when Alex and I broke up, I didn't really think about him seeing someone else. But now I know why he couldn't talk to me last night."

"You called him?" I asked.

She nodded. "He said he couldn't talk, that it was too hard for him. But now I see why. Gretchen was probably there."

"Not necessarily," Erin said. "Besides, Gretchen can't mean half as much to him as you do. You and Alex can still get back together if that's what you want."

Jessica shook her head. "I don't know what I want," she said.

"Come on, let's go," Erin said, gently turning Jessica around so she couldn't see Alex. "I think it's time for a trip to the food court."

When Erin and I got back to my house a few hours later, I was surprised to see Betty in the kitchen.

"Your father asked me to stay over tonight and tomorrow," she explained. "He had to go out of town, but he left this for you." She handed me a white envelope.

Inside was a note from my dad and fifty dollars. He'd left me money for concert souvenirs and gas, and told me to have a great time with Kerri. He'd signed it, "lots of love, Dad."

I touched the edge of the note. All of a sudden I felt guilty for lying to him about who I was taking to the concert. There was no reason my dad shouldn't know about Luke. I mean, I should probably get him used to the fact that I wanted to date—especially when we had vowed to be totally honest with each other.

*I'll tell him on Sunday,* I decided as Erin began taking out our purchases and tossing them on the family room couch.

*From now on,* I promised myself, *I'll be the daughter he thinks I am. For real.*

At about midnight, I switched off the TV and got ready for bed. Just before I turned off the light, my phone rang.

*Strange,* I thought. *Maybe it's Dad.* I reached over to my nightstand and picked up the phone. I had a private line, so I was pretty sure the call wouldn't wake Betty.

"Hello?" I said.

"Hi, Maya." It was a boy's voice.

"Who is this?"

"It's Jared. Jared Mason. You know me. I'm a friend of T.J.'s."

I remembered Jared. He was a big guy with white-blond hair and ruddy skin. He'd been at Turtle's party.

"What do you want?" I asked nervously.

"Listen, do you want to do something with me tomorrow night?" Jared said. "I'll pick you up in my car. We can go for a drive."

I struggled to keep my voice calm. "I'm busy tomorrow night."

"That's okay," he said in a smarmy voice. "I'll see you some other time. T.J. told me all about you. You sound like the kind of girl I like."

I heard laughter in the background—a whole gang of boys. My heart started racing. T.J. was with him, I just knew it.

I hung up without saying another word. Then I huddled in bed, shaking.

Where were they calling from? Did they know that my dad wasn't around? That it was just Betty and me in the house?

A few seconds later, the phone rang again. I ignored it, got out of bed, and ran through the house, checking to make sure all the doors and windows were locked.

The phone stopped ringing. I got back into bed.

After another minute, it started ringing again.

I unplugged the phone. I left the light on and cowered under the covers all night long.

It was exactly two hours before I had to leave for the concert, and I was staring at my reflection in my bedroom mirror. The outfit had looked so great in the store: the embroidered jeans, the cute little peasant blouse, the delicate necklace.

So how come it looked so different now? The jeans fit my legs like a wetsuit, the shirt was too small, and the necklace looked cheap.

And I was tired. I hadn't slept well last night. I had called Erin and told her about the phone call first thing in the morning, and she convinced me that the boys were probably just trying to scare me. It had worked.

I tried to put it out of my mind as I pushed the speed-dial button for Erin. I had a date to worry about.

Erin picked up on the first ring.

"I look awful!" I wailed.

"What happened to hello?" she replied.

I groaned. "Erin, you don't understand. Everything we bought at the mall is wrong! Nothing looks right. It's all too sexy."

"Ah, that's a real problem for a girl going out

on a date," Erin said.

I paced back and forth. "Erin, I'm serious."

Erin's tone softened. "I know, Maya. I'm sorry. It's just that I'm trying to get ready for my date with Sam. Why, though, is beyond me. I know I'm going to have a rotten time."

Sam, aka Shoe Store Guy, had sent Erin an e-mail, and they'd agreed to meet at a Starbucks downtown.

I knew I was being a pest, but I couldn't help it. "I'm so nervous! Nothing looks good on me."

"What about the cords and that brown button-down shirt?" Erin suggested.

"Tried 'em. Hated 'em."

"The blue dress?"

"Slut city."

Erin sighed. "Maya, you're going to look nice in whatever you wear. There's no way Luke is going to get the wrong impression. Did you see some of the outfits on the MTV awards? *Those* clothes are revealing. The stuff we bought isn't even close."

"I guess," I said, although I still didn't know what I was going to wear. "Okay. Thanks."

"You're welcome."

I hung up and wandered over to my bed, using the remote to crank up my CD player. Jeans, halters, shirts—everything from our shopping trip and more from my closet was spread out over the bed. I rummaged through the pile. Nothing was even close to right.

As the music blasted through my speakers, I drifted out into the silent hallway. I'd gotten so used to having all Dad's advisers in the house that it felt strangely vacant. Empty.

My bare feet moved down the plush cream carpeting. I stopped outside the door to my parents' room. Even though my mom had been gone for twenty-two months, I still thought of it as *their* room. Flipping on the light switch, I crossed the threshold. Everything was tidy. Perfect. The king-size bed, its pillows plump in masculine shades of hunter green and burgundy. The framed print of the coast of Maine that hung above the bed. On the nightstand, the legal thriller Dad was reading.

There was no sign that a woman had ever inhabited this room. My dad had wanted it that way when he'd had it completely redecorated after my mom's death. But he'd left her walk-in closet untouched. I crossed over to it and turned on the light. All her clothes—her dresses and skirts, blouses on puffy satin hangers and shoes on racks—remained.

I closed my eyes and breathed deeply. If I concentrated hard enough, I could smell the perfume she wore, the sachets that scented her sweaters. My fingers reached out and grazed her fuzzy white bathrobe, then a blazer, then a silk shirt. Opening my eyes, I lifted a sleeveless black cashmere sweater from the shelf. I could still see my mom in this; she'd worn it on our last good New Year's Eve, the last one before she was diagnosed.

I brought the sweater to my cheek, blinking back tears as I remembered how pretty she had looked that night. Clutching the sweater to my chest, I turned off the light and headed back to my room. I'd found what I wanted to wear after all.

# Chapter 10

**"T**his is my favorite place to see a band," Luke said as we took our seats at the Flare. "I hate those big arena shows."

I nodded, looking around. The Flare was an old theater that attracted the top bands on the college circuit. I'd never been there before, but I liked the funky black curtains that draped from the ceiling and the gargoyles that studded the side walls.

Luke had been sitting on a bench at the corner where we'd arranged to meet. I'd managed to say hello, but that was about it. I was so nervous! My stomach was filled with butterflies, and I was sure I was going to do or say something totally, completely wrong.

The sight of him waiting for me in his jeans and a close-fitting T-shirt, his hair curling around his neck, had sent goose bumps down my arms. I wasn't sure if it was because I was scared or because I was attracted to him. Maybe a little of both.

Of course, I'd been extremely nervous on the way to the concert. I kept thinking up different scenarios. What if he wanted to kiss me? What if he wanted to do more? What if he was a jerk? What if he was nice? But talking to Dr. Sheridan about it had given me some confidence. I told myself that whatever came up, I could handle it.

"Who else have you seen here?" I asked him now, trying to come up with something to say.

"The Bug Rockets," Luke replied. "And Tanker. I guess I've only been here twice before." He smiled shyly, as if I'd caught him boasting. "If I ever get a band together, I'd love to play here."

"Do you play an instrument?" I asked.

"Well, I'm learning to play keyboard. I'm not very good yet, but I'd like to be in a band. Everybody wants to be a rock star, right?"

"I don't," I said.

"What do you want to do?" he asked.

"I don't know," I confessed. "I mean, I'm not sure what I want to do—but my dad has it all figured out for me. Law, law, law. I don't think he even realizes that there are other career options. Like, I was really into my biology class last year. Maybe I could do something with that." *Why am I telling him this?* I asked myself. *It sounds so stupid. I should just shut up.*

"My dad is pretty cool about that stuff," Luke told me. "He knows I'm really into music. If I go to college I want to major in music and play the bar circuit at night."

A thrill went through me as the lights went off, the band came on, and the crowd went wild. Luke jumped up and pulled me to my feet. As the lights began flashing on the stage, Luke bent his head close to mine. "This is so cool," he said, his breath warm in my ear. "I'm really glad you asked me to come."

"Me too," I said shyly, trying not to freak out over the fact that we were holding hands.

Hearing the music loosened me up, and with each song I grew a little more relaxed. We were on our feet for almost the entire concert, dancing to every song.

When the last encore ended, we were still holding hands. Luke had let go only to clap and buy me a soda at intermission. Other than that, I felt the soft pressure of his palm for the entire concert. The weirdest part was, I felt amazingly relaxed. It was as if we'd done this lots of times before.

As we filed out of the hall, Luke said, "Where to next? Want to head over to Pizza Pi or the Cellar?"

I hesitated. I'd told Betty that I'd come straight home after the concert. But I *was* having a good time. And Luke really did seem nice. I thought I could like him . . . if I let myself.

"Or would you rather go somewhere quiet, where we could talk?"

Just as I was about to answer, a drunk Oneida fan pushed past us and sloshed beer all over us.

"Thanks a lot," Luke muttered, shaking his head. He tried to wipe off the beer with his hands, but his jeans were soaked.

"Are you okay?" I asked.

"Yeah. Just sticky." He brushed off his hands. "So what do you think?"

"Let's go somewhere quiet," I said.

"Okay." We walked out into the lobby.

"I just have to make a couple of phone calls," I said, taking out my cell phone and walking over to an empty corner where I could hear better. First I called Betty, and told her that I was going to get something to eat. Then I dialed Kerri's pager number. A minute later, she called me back. "Where are you?" she said, her voice muffled. "We're on the bus back to school. We won!"

I quickly told her how well the night was going, stealing glances at Luke as I did. I didn't want him to know I was talking about him, and I felt silly checking in with Kerri after he'd been so nice. Still, it felt good to hear her voice. We made plans to meet for breakfast at her place the next morning. She said she'd leave messages for Erin and Jessica to come too. "I want to hear everything!" Kerri insisted before we hung up.

I went back to Luke. "Sorry. I promised Kerri I'd call her," I explained.

"No problem," he said. "It gave me time to think about where I want to take you." Between Luke's soft voice and his intense, dark eyes, I was feeling kind of dazzled. Not only was he cute, he was thoughtful. I was glad I'd given this a chance.

When we got outside, I found out Luke had taken the bus to the concert. If we were going to go somewhere, we'd have to go in my car. When Luke saw the BMW, he let out a low whistle.

"Wow! Awesome wheels," he said, running his fingers over the shining silver hood.

"I got it for my sixteenth birthday," I explained, slightly embarrassed. I didn't want him to think I was some rich snob.

"I've never driven anything besides my dad's Camry," Luke confessed with a laugh.

I paused. "You can drive if you want to," I blurted out.

His eyes lit up. "Your Beamer? You're sure?"

I nodded.

"I won't ask twice." He opened my door and then went to the driver's side and got in.

It was a little weird being a passenger in my own car. But Luke handled the BMW great. I thought it was cute how careful he was being.

"I've got the perfect place to take you," he said as we drove away from the lights of the concert hall and onto the highway.

"Where?"

He shook his head evasively. "You'll see."

"Okay," I said as I settled back in my seat. I tried to think where we might be going. Not Pizza Pi, not the Cellar. Bernie's would be closed. Starbucks wasn't quiet.

I guess I was picturing us going to some little café, but we weren't heading toward the downtown area at all.

"The lake?" I asked, starting to feel kind of nervous. Kids went there to make out. I definitely didn't want to go there.

"Not the lake," he said mischievously. "You'll never guess."

My heart started to speed up as Luke kept driving. It went into a full pounding hammer when he exited off onto a dark, deserted stretch of road. *Should I tell him to turn back?* I wondered. *Would I seem like an idiot? Would he even listen?*

"Luke," I began. "I don't know where—"

"It's a surprise," he said. "Trust me."

We were the only car on the road now. The BMW's headlights cast creepy shadows on the trees that lined the route as we drove farther and farther from Madison. I could feel my throat tightening with fear.

I gripped the armrest as the car sped into the night. Where were we going? What had I gotten myself into?

# Chapter 11

**W**hen Luke pulled the car into the empty parking lot of Lipcott's Fun World, I was so frightened I could barely speak. For the past few minutes I'd been convinced he was going to pull off onto some dead-end dirt road and attack me.

Now, as I tried to breathe evenly, I wondered why he'd brought me here. The old-fashioned family amusement park was a local tradition; there wasn't a kid in Madison who hadn't begged his or her parents to go out to Lipcott's at least once a week in the summer. But summer was over. The park was closed for the season now.

"Here we are," Luke said, turning off the engine and getting out. "Come on."

I sat there, not moving, not wanting to give up the safety of my car.

"Maya, is something wrong?" Luke asked, bending down to look at me.

"No . . . nothing's wrong," I said, trying to force a smile.

Luke gestured to the park. "I know, I know. You probably think I'm some weirdo, bringing you here." He shrugged. "What can I tell you? It's my favorite place." He offered me his hand. "Will you come with me?"

Somehow his asking me made me calmer—like I *did* have a choice in the matter. Gulping, I got out of the car, and took his hand as we walked across the parking lot. "Uh, Luke, I think they're closed," I said, glancing around us.

"Not for season ticket holders like me," he said, grinning. We approached the marquee at the main entrance. BE PREPARED FOR THE THRILL OF A LIFETIME! it read.

"I worked here for the past two summers," Luke explained. "And it's a known fact that the guys who work at Lipcott's bring girls here after hours. All you have to do is hop the fence, and it's extra low over here." He walked over to the mesh wire.

"What about the 'No Trespassing' sign?" I asked uneasily, wondering how many girls Luke had brought to the park before me.

"How can you have the thrill of a lifetime if you don't break the rules?" Luke asked with a smile. He helped boost me over, and then hopped down to join me on the other side.

It was eerie being in the park at night, without any other people, without the whir of the rides and the blinking lights of the midway casting their glow. I never liked being in deserted places. Once I'd been with Jessica at the mall and she'd left her wallet in a store. We'd had to go back to the mall office to get it when the rest of the mall was closed. I hated walking through the deserted corridors, our footsteps echoing on the tiles. I was sure something terrible was going to happen.

Now Luke and I walked past the empty food vending booths, and the Fun or Run House with the ghoulish figures that stood sentry at its entrance, spooky in the shadows.

"I wish we could ride the Green Streak," Luke said as we approached the park's classic wooden roller coaster, its cars covered up for the winter.

"You like roller coasters?" I asked.

"Love them," he said.

I smiled. "Me too. The more loops the better."

"I never would have guessed that about you," Luke said. "You seem more like a Ferris wheel girl."

We turned down one of the main passages. It was brighter here, with slivers of moonlight lighting our way. Luke pointed to a ride just ahead. "This is where I worked."

"The Fuller Carousel?" I asked. "This was always my favorite!"

We walked up to the low iron gate that surrounded the carousel and let ourselves in. The Fuller Carousel was one of the most beautiful merry-go-rounds I'd ever seen. The horses were painted in beautiful bright colors—pink, turquoise, magenta, yellow—and trimmed with silver. The top of the carousel was rimmed with heavy gold-framed mirrors and small paintings of ponies and riders. When I was little I always wanted to ride the turquoise horse with the golden mane.

The horses were covered with tarps, but Luke quickly undraped two of them. I felt a little better when I saw that one of them was my familiar turquoise friend.

After helping me onto my horse, he climbed up on the other.

"So how would you normally be spending a Friday night?" Luke asked. "With your friends?"

I shrugged. "Not lately. Kerri's usually with Matt or working, and Jessica's always studying. Erin and I hang out a lot, but lately she's been tied up with drama club stuff." I put my feet in the stirrups. "So most Saturday nights, I watch movies and get my homework done for Monday," I said. "Lame, huh?"

"What's so lame about it?" Luke said. "I think

everybody at school likes to make it sound like they have this wild social life or something when really, they're sitting home watching MTV and eating Doritos."

"My father doesn't like me to watch MTV," I said. "He says it's a bad influence. I watch it, but if he comes into the room I switch channels. He's pretty overprotective." I leaned my head against the pole. "He's going to be running for lieutenant governor of Wisconsin."

Luke whistled. "That must be intense."

"Yeah," I said.

"My dad works for FarmCor—they manufacture farming machinery. It's not what you'd call a high-profile job."

"You're lucky. My dad's under a lot of pressure, and he winds up putting the pressure on me," I explained. "It's hard. And ever since my mom . . ." I stopped. I never liked talking about my mom, especially with people I didn't know well. But I couldn't just leave my words hanging. "She died two years ago. Cancer."

Luke hesitated. "My mom's been gone four years. I still wake up thinking she's going to be there in the kitchen when I go downstairs."

He looked down at the ground, then gazed up at me. *He knows what it's like,* I thought, looking back at him. For the first time I realized that maybe a guy really *could* understand what I was going through.

I cleared my throat. "Boy, we sure know how to liven up a date," I said.

Luke grinned. "It's good to talk about that kind of stuff, though," he said. "I mean, sometimes. Four years ago, I thought I'd never be able to say the word 'mother' without . . . you know . . ." He paused, embarrassed.

It was weird, but Dr. Sheridan popped into my mind at that moment. I thought about how much it was helping me to have her to talk to. How talking to her seemed to give me the confidence to open up to people.

"But there's something about you, Maya," Luke went on. "I had a feeling I'd be able to talk to you."

I rested my head on the horse's brass pole, glad he couldn't see me blushing in the dark.

"But I was afraid to ask you out," Luke admitted. "You kind of seemed to be avoiding me. I thought you must have a boyfriend."

"I . . . no," I said, wondering if he'd heard any of the rumors T.J. had spread. "I just . . . didn't think I wanted a boyfriend."

"Do you think you want one now?" he asked. He leaned forward and smiled as if he was auditioning for the part.

I giggled, my nerves on edge. "I don't know. Maybe."

"I'm glad." He leaned closer, his lips inches from my own.

Suddenly my heart felt icy. *Should I trust him?* I wondered anxiously, my fingers gripping the brass pole. The moonlight, the carousel, the gentle night breeze—everything seemed right for a romantic kiss. But still, I pulled back.

"What's the matter, Maya?" Luke asked. "Did I do something wrong? Do you want to go back to the car?"

*He's really concerned about me*, I realized as I looked into his eyes. I took a deep breath and shook my head. Luke *was* different—way different from T.J. I didn't need to pull away. And I didn't want to. Leaning forward, I touched my lips to his.

Luke's mouth was warm and sweet, and I found myself melting into him, loving how wonderful he felt. Kissing him was nothing like kissing T.J. that night at the party. Kissing Luke felt right and perfect and totally, completely comfortable.

It was the kind of kiss I'd been waiting for my whole life.

"So what's your curfew?" Luke asked as we walked across the deserted parking lot to the car.

"Nine on school nights, eleven on weekends," I said, glancing at my watch. "I don't really go out all that much."

"Me neither," Luke said, unlocking the doors. "But I hope that will change—now that there's somebody I want to go out with."

A shiver of excitement ran through me as I slipped into the passenger seat once more.

Luke got behind the wheel.

"I wish we didn't have to go yet," I said as the clock on my dashboard blinked 10:30.

Luke reached over and touched my cheek. "Do you have time for one more kiss?" he asked softly.

I nodded.

This kiss was even better than the first. My stomach was all tingly, and when Luke put his hands on my shoulders, I felt ready to melt.

*This has been the most perfect night of my life,* I thought.

"I really like you, Maya," Luke whispered. Then our lips met again, and it was pure bliss . . . until a glaring white light shone in through the windshield.

We pulled apart, startled, as someone rapped hard on the window. "Open up! This is the police!"

# Chapter 12

'll need to see your registration and your license," the officer told Luke. He leaned over to look at me. "Yours too."

"Actually this is her car," Luke said as I fumbled through the papers in the glove compartment. My hands were shaking as I opened a small vinyl envelope and hurriedly flipped through the contents.

"I'll still need to see your license," the cop told Luke. "And your registration, license, and proof of insurance, Miss."

But I couldn't find the registration. "Here's my license and the insurance card," I said as I handed them over.

The cop frowned as he took them. "You can't drive a car without a registration."

"I know. I . . . I . . ." I stammered. "My dad takes care of it. I thought he kept the registration in here—"

"Here's my license," Luke blurted out. The cop

took it and told us to wait in the car while he went back to his patrol car, where another officer waited.

"He's gonna run a license plate check," Luke said under his breath.

"Do you think he thinks we stole my car?" I asked, panicked. "I mean, I know there aren't a lot of kids driving brand-new BMWs around Madison."

"Nah. It's routine." Luke looked worried. "I don't think he was too cool with your not having the registration, though."

"At least we had our licenses," I said, staring down at my leather wallet.

But when the officer finally came back with his partner, their faces were grim. "You two are going to have to come with us down to the station."

"What for?" I asked, trying not to cry.

The cop that had taken our IDs looked at me. "For starters, no registration. Then we have breaking and entering the park."

"But—" Luke tried to protest.

"And," the cop went on, ignoring him, "you both are under the age of twenty-one and smell of alcohol."

"But . . ." I started to explain, but I wondered if they'd believe me when I told them about the beer that had spilled all over Luke at the concert.

"You can explain at the station," the first cop said.

They gave us each a Breathalyzer test—which we both passed. But they still wanted to take us to the police station for questioning.

Feeling helpless and sick with dread, I followed Luke to the patrol car. *Please,* I prayed silently, *don't let my dad ever find out about this.*

The on-duty police at the station asked us both a lot of questions about where we'd been and what we were doing at Lipcott's. Then, without a hint of what was to come, they made Luke and me wait in a small, brightly lit room. The only furniture was a couple of plastic orange chairs and a cheap wooden conference table covered with coffee mug stains.

Luke stared up at the ceiling and let out a breath. "I'm really sorry, Maya," he said. "I never would have taken you there if I thought we were going to get into trouble."

"It's not your fault," I said, wrapping my arms around my chest and willing myself to be strong.

We both looked up when the door opened, and an officer motioned us out. "In there," he said, pointing to a dingy room crowded with desks and file cabinets. A male cop sat at one of the desks. A woman in a police uniform was on the phone at another desk, and a skinny man in a wrinkled shirt and pants—who I guessed was a detective—sat in front of her, working on a crossword puzzle.

We sat down in front of the male cop. His badge said he was Sergeant Willis. In front of him was Luke's driver's license. "Trespassing, no registration. Not looking good, kiddies."

Luke swallowed. "Like we told the other officer, we . . . we just wanted to be alone."

"So you hopped a fence and made yourselves at home at Lipcott's?" Willis asked.

"What are you going to do to us?" I asked, nervously spinning the ruby ring on my finger. I couldn't take much more of this suspense.

The sergeant eyed me. "Well, considering that young Mr. Perez here passed the Breathalyzer test, he will be given a warning and released." He drummed his pencil on the table. "Now you, Miss Greer, we have a slight problem with you."

I gripped the armrests of my chair.

"We're going to have to phone your father and see if he can bring the car registration down to the precinct."

"No!" I gasped. "Oh, please, please don't call him."

The sergeant gave a weary sigh. "Believe me, I've heard it all. But tell me anyway. Why shouldn't we call your father?"

"Because . . . because he's the district attorney and something like this would make a lot of trouble for him," I blurted out.

The skinny detective with the crossword puzzle sat up straight. "You're DA Greer's kid?" he asked.

I nodded. I wanted to ask what business was it of his who I was, but I didn't dare. I didn't want to say anything that might make Sergeant Willis angrier than he was.

The sergeant tossed his pencil back and forth. "So, you're the DA's kid, huh?" He looked at me. "Well, since you haven't been drinking—although you both reek like a brewery . . ." He wrinkled his nose. "I guess I can let this go."

"Oh, thank you!" I told him.

He held up a finger. "Under one condition. You bring me that registration tomorrow."

"I will," I promised.

Sergeant Willis told me where I could find my car. Then he gazed at Luke. "Let's hope we don't meet again," he said.

As we walked outside, I'd never been so glad to see the moon and stars in my life. As soon as I got home, I pulled out my journal:

Saturday, 2 am
Totally incredible night! (Hope Betty doesn't tell Dad what time I got home—yikes!) I don't even know where to start. I mean, yesterday my life seemed so boring and now it's like, full of adventure! I kind of feel

like a butterfly popping out of her cocoon. Very corny, I know. Can't help it. I feel so giddy. Happy for once. I just want to jump on my bed, and laugh and scream!

I'm so glad that my friends convinced me to go out with Luke. Yeah, it was a little weird at first when he held my hand at the Oneida concert, but by the end of the show I never wanted to let go.

Now I feel kind of stupid for getting scared in the car on the way to Lipcott's. Guess I thought that Luke was going to be just like T.J. That maybe he'd heard what T.J. and his crew keep saying about me, and wanted to find out if it was true. But I think I was wrong about that—and I've never been so psyched to be wrong!

Luke was so sweet tonight. And when he told me about his mom and how much he misses her—I felt this kind of bond with him. I mean, he's the first person (aside from Dr. Sheridan) that I could really open up to about my mom's death. Dad never wants to talk about her, and even though my friends are totally there for me, they don't know what it's like to lose someone you really, really love. To see your mom slowly fade away and die.

It's strange, but somehow I think Mom was watching over me tonight. I think she saw me get my first real kiss (which was incredible!). And I'm glad about that. Really glad.

But the police station I could live without anyone knowing about. God, if Dad ever finds out . . . Well, I'll have to tell him. But at least he won't hear it from the police. Have to tell him about Luke too, I guess. I know he'd like Luke if he met him.

I don't know why, but I feel so close to Luke now after only one date. All my instincts tell me that he's a great guy. I just hope I'm not being fooled somehow. That Luke really likes me as much as I like him.

The sun streamed through the stained-glass windows Sunday morning, sending patterns of color along the pews of Our Lady of Hope, the local church where I try to attend Mass on a semi-regular basis. I didn't really consider myself a super-religious person, but there was something about attending services that I found soothing. It wasn't that I thought you could go out and do all sorts of bad things and then come to Mass or confession and be absolved. I guess it was more that being here listening to the prayers and hearing the music made me feel at peace with myself.

When my mom was alive, we'd attended pretty regularly. Being in the church reminded me of her. I even prayed to her here. I knew it was kind of dumb . . . here were all these people praying to God and the saints, and I was praying to my dead mother. But it made me feel better. I'd gone to her grave a couple of times, but I didn't like being there, thinking of her casket buried under the cold, hard earth. It was much better to think of her here, in a place she loved.

After the service I lit a candle, then said a silent prayer of thanks before retrieving my coat from the rack and walking out into the sunshine. Last night I'd been so scared that my dad was going to find out about the police incident, but when I woke up this morning, the first thing I did was head over to the police station to show Sergeant Willis my registration, which I'd found in my dad's desk. Then on the way here, when I realized it was over, relief had literally poured over me.

It was still bright and early when I pulled my car into the Dunkin' Donuts shop on the way to Kerri's house. The place was filled with the Sunday morning crowd, and I had to wait in line, the smell of fresh doughnuts making my stomach rumble. All I could think about was how I couldn't wait to tell Kerri what had happened last night.

I shifted impatiently, my eyes roaming the store. I'm always restless when I have to wait in line. I looked over the doughnut selection, trying to decide what to pick. Kerri always liked gooey ones. I was more of a chocolate-glazed girl myself.

A man behind me stepped forward to pick up the *Madison Herald*, and jostled my arm. "Sorry," he apologized.

I smiled. "That's okay." There was a huge stack of papers piled on a table near the counter. I wasn't surprised to see my last name was on the front page. Seeing the name Greer in print barely registered with me anymore. My dad had been in the paper a lot since he became district attorney.

As I got closer, I zeroed in on the front-page headline: "DA Greer's Daughter No Angel!"

"Oh, my god," I gasped, grabbing a paper. There, in black and white, were the details of my date with Luke! Words such as "trespassing," "minors," and "drinking" leaped out at me.

*How did it get into the newspaper?* I wondered. I had no idea.

In a daze, I dropped the paper onto the stack and stumbled out of the line, pushing open the store's heavy glass door.

My father had always said the media twisted the facts. But I wasn't so sure he would see it that way when it applied to me. For one desperate second I thought of running back inside and buying all the newspapers, trying to keep the news from leaking out. But there was no way this was going to get past my dad. What was this going to do to his campaign?

I got back into my car and just sat there, tears running down my face. *I am so dead,* I thought.

# Chapter 13

**K**erri and Erin sat in the Hopkinses' living room, staring at the Sunday paper.

"Have you spoken to Luke since this came out?" Kerri asked as I collapsed on her couch.

"No!" I cried. And I didn't want to. The humiliation was finally hitting me. First T.J.'s awful rumors, and now this? "And wait until my dad finds out. He's going to be so angry. He'll never let me out of the house again," I whispered, burying my tear-stained face in a velour pillow.

Erin perched beside me. "But you guys didn't really do anything that bad. The newspaper just twisted the facts."

"Yeah, but who cares about the facts? The headline is what everyone's going to remember," I said bitterly. I tried to smile, but my quivering chin gave me away. "My father's going to disown me," I whispered, fresh tears filling my eyes.

Kerri's mom and Kerri's older brother, Dan, came into the living room. "Maya, you should see this," Liz said soberly, turning on the TV. She was still in her robe. "We were watching the news on the TV in the kitchen."

I gasped as the image flickered into focus. There was my father at the fancy hotel where he had brunch sometimes, surrounded by cameras and being interrogated by reporters.

"Mr. Greer," one reporter called out, "are you or are you not running for lieutenant governor?"

"I haven't made that decision yet," my father replied.

"What makes you think you can be second in command for the state when you can't even control your own daughter?" another reporter called.

"Oh, no!" I groaned. "He's going to kill me!"

But my dad's reply surprised me. "My daughter's private life is not the public's business," he answered in a perfectly calm tone. "She is a private citizen, and her actions should not fall under the media spotlight that surrounds me. I trust her, and I'm sure that this incident was blown completely out of proportion. Thank you." The camera panned over to a blond reporter.

"There you have it, folks. With rumors swirling over DA Greer's possible run for lieutenant governor, every action counts—in this case, even the actions of District Attorney Greer's teenage daughter. I'm Shelley Fitz. Now, back to you, Lou."

"That wasn't so bad!" Kerri said as Dan turned the TV off. "He told them where to go!"

Erin put her arm around my shoulders. "Your dad really stood up for you."

"He loves you, Maya," Liz said. "He's going to understand."

I wiped the tears from my face. Maybe they were right. In a way it was better that my dad already knew. I didn't know how I'd ever been able to muster up the courage to tell him. And he did sound very calm about it. Maybe things would be okay.

As Liz and Dan returned to the kitchen, Kerri curled up on the other end of the sofa. "Okay, now I want the good stuff. How was your date?"

I managed to smile for real this time. "It was wonderful." I told them everything, from the concert to the amusement park to the way Luke was so gentle and sweet when he kissed me.

Kerri hopped up and did a little victory dance. "I knew he was right for you!"

"How was *your* date?" I asked Erin, remembering for the first time that she'd gone out with Shoe Store Sam.

She groaned, flipping back her pigtails. "There's

a reason he works at a shoe store. The guy loves feet. He can't get enough of them."

"What are you talking about?" Kerri asked.

"Remember the first thing he said to me? 'Your feet are so small,' right? He didn't stop looking at my feet all night. Or talking about feet. Which movie stars have the best feet. How most models' feet are as big as flippers. How he could never date a girl who wore bigger than a size seven shoe."

"Bizarre," I said, wrinkling my nose.

"That's one guy I never have to worry about," Kerri said with a laugh, waggling her size nines.

"Is it me?" Erin said. "Do I do something to attract these weirdoes?"

Liz poked her head around the corner. "Maya, if you want, I'll take you home when you're ready. It could be a mob scene at your house," she warned. "You might not want to face that alone."

"You don't have to," I told her. I appreciated her offer, but the reporters weren't really interested in me . . . it was my dad they wanted, and he'd already spoken to them. *And he did a great job*, I reminded myself.

Since I'd run out of the doughnut shop without the doughnuts, Kerri, Erin, and I decided to make omelets. It was almost noon before we ate, and one by the time I said good-bye and went home. When I reached the castle, I recognized Marlene's car in the driveway, along with those of a few of the staffers.

Before I'd even put my key in the front door, it opened. My father stood there. And he did not look happy.

"Where have you been?" he demanded.

"At Kerri's," I said nervously. "Sorry I forgot to tell Betty I was going after church. We were just hanging out."

"Is that what you were doing last night with Luke Perez?"

I swallowed. Uh-oh. Where was the calm, supportive dad I had seen on TV? He'd been so great with the reporters. What happened to "My daughter's personal life is her own business and I trust her"?

"Don't you understand what something like this could do to my campaign?" he asked me.

I just shook my head, feeling helpless.

He motioned for me to join him in the kitchen, where Marlene was pacing back and forth, yakking away on her cell phone. Newspapers were spread over the kitchen table, all of them featuring me. Marlene saw us and clicked off. "How could you have been so careless?" she demanded, slamming the phone on the counter.

I blinked, taken aback. "I didn't mean—"

"We were totally caught off guard when the press

ambushed us this morning," she scolded. Her voice rose with each syllable. "Your father is going to have to spend the next few weeks backpedaling and hoping that this all blows over! Not to mention the questions that are sure to come up during the big speech he has to give on Tuesday, where your attendance is mandatory," she finished, crossing her arms.

Several members of my father's staff had stopped to gawk at us. I couldn't take this kind of humiliation in my own home. Who did she think she was, laying into me like that?

I lost it. "Last time I checked, Marlene, you weren't my mother. If my dad has a problem, it's up to him to let me know." I glared at them both. "But as usual, he's much too busy."

"That's enough!" my father snapped.

"I'm sorry," Marlene apologized to me. "It's been a little tense here today." She turned to my dad. "I'll be in the living room if you need me," she said, heading out of the kitchen.

My dad shook his head. "Maya, you lied to me. You told me you were going to the concert with Kerri, and instead you were with some boy I don't even know."

I blinked back tears. "I know, Dad. I know I was wrong. But I didn't mean to do anything that would hurt anybody."

He cut me off. "You have never, ever been in any trouble. But suddenly you're breaking the law by trespassing. You smelled of booze, and you were out way past your curfew." He paused. "Not to mention lying to me after we had an agreement. An honesty agreement, Maya." He slammed his hand on the counter. "You are not to see this boy again."

"Wait a minute, Dad," I said. "Just because you're mad at me, that doesn't mean you have to take it out on Luke. He wasn't to blame. He didn't—"

"Maya, don't argue with me now." My father's eyes were full of disappointment. "You've clearly shown me that I can't trust you. I thought I could, but I was wrong."

"You *can* trust me!" I cried. "You're the one who always says the newspapers distort things. If you'd just let me explain—"

"End of discussion," my father said. "I don't want you seeing him."

"I can't believe you!" I shouted, rage boiling up inside me. "I finally find a guy I like and you want to ban him from my life? You're not being fair!"

"You go on one date with him, and you wind up in police custody. What more do I need to know?" my father snorted.

"But you don't even know him."

"This isn't open for discussion," my dad said. "I

think I made myself perfectly clear. You're not to see him again. And you are grounded until Friday."

I ran upstairs, taking the steps two at a time. My eyes were streaming as I ran into my room and grabbed my journal from my desk drawer. I went into my bathroom, slammed the door behind me and locked it for good measure.

Dear Dad,

You are so unfair! You're not even giving me a chance to explain what happened. I know what I did was wrong, and if you could read my mind, you'd know how bad I've felt about lying to you, about keeping ANYTHING from you after we promised each other to be honest.

I know you love me . . . and that's why I'm sure that if you knew what had gone on between me and T.J. and how I've been feeling about guys lately, you'd be glad that I had a date . . . a good date!

No matter what you say, I'm not going to stop seeing Luke. He's the best thing that's happened to me all senior year.

So don't make me give him up.

Because I'm telling you . . . I won't.

# Chapter 14

**I** braced myself before I stepped inside the school on Monday morning. *Okay,* I thought, taking a deep breath. *Here I go.* I felt as if I was about to step into a war zone—me versus everybody else.

It turned out to be worse than I expected.

As soon as I entered the building, all eyes turned to me. Everybody stared as I walked down the hall. I hunched over, wishing I could shrivel up and die.

And once I passed by, they started whispering. Little bits of gossip reached me as I slunk through the halls.

"I wonder how many other guys she sneaks out with."

"I never knew she was so wild. She always seemed so quiet."

"T.J. must have been telling the truth!"

Jimmy Wright and Brian Robinson, two of T.J.'s friends, sidled up to me, one on either side. "Hey,

Maya—you're famous!" Jimmy said with a leer.

"Hey, Maya, any time you want to get together, give me a call," Brian said. "I heard you're a lot of fun."

My heart thumping, I pushed past them. What could I say to them? Now everybody would believe T.J.'s lies—because they'd read about me in the paper!

I hurried around the corner. Kerri, Erin, and Jessica were huddled outside Erin's homeroom.

"So there's this guy in Study Hall who's been totally flirting with me . . ." Erin was saying.

"Can I die now?" I said as I joined them. "The whole school thinks I'm . . . I'm . . . I don't know what!"

"They're all morons," Kerri said, giving me a sympathetic look. "What's going on with your dad? Are you still grounded?"

I'd e-mailed them about my dad's reaction to the newspapers.

"Yes. And I can't see Luke again. He's not going to change his mind," I said.

I glanced up and saw Alex approaching. Jessica followed my gaze.

"Hey, Jess, can I talk to you for a minute?" Alex asked.

"Sure," Jessica replied, nervously tucking her

hair behind her ear.

Kerri, Erin, and I watched as they crossed the hall and leaned against some of the gray lockers that lined the hallway. Even with all the noise in the hall, we could still pick up some of their conversation.

"Um . . . Jess . . . I'm not sure we can keep being friends," Alex told her.

Jessica looked stunned. "Why?"

"It's just too hard. Every time I see you or talk to you, it hurts. I need a clean break, Jess."

"What did he just say?" Erin whispered.

"What you thought he said," Kerri said grimly. "He doesn't want to see her or talk to her anymore."

Jessica's face twitched. I could tell she was fighting back tears. "Can we talk about this some-where else?" she asked him.

Alex shook his head. "I've got to go." He turned and walked down the hall.

Jessica came back over to us, her face ashen. "Alex says he can't be my friend anymore," she whispered, her voice shaking. "When we broke up, I never thought . . ." She choked back a huge sob. "I never thought that we wouldn't be friends anymore."

We wanted to console her more than anything, but the bell was ringing and we had to get to class. "If I don't see you later, call me tonight," I told her. I wasn't sure if she was going to make it to chorus today—not with the way she was feeling, anyway.

I found Luke waiting for me at my locker just before lunch. His eyes had a serious expression. I wondered if he'd gotten into trouble because of the newspaper story.

"That was some article," he said.

"Could you believe it?" I moaned. "I sure couldn't."

"My dad thought the whole thing was kind of funny," Luke said, offering me a smile. "My friends have been teasing me too."

I wrapped my arms around myself. "My dad didn't find it funny. I'm grounded for a week."

Luke frowned. "That's awful."

"And that's not all," I said. "He doesn't want me to see you anymore. We had a big fight about it, and I lost." I glanced at Luke, feeling utterly hopeless. "Once my dad says something, that's it. There's no way he's going to change his mind."

"But I really want to keep seeing you," Luke said, sending shivers up my back. "I like you, Maya. I like you a lot."

A wave of happiness washed over me. It was good to know he liked me—even if I couldn't see him.

"There's got to be a way to fix this," Luke added.

"We'll figure something out. I promise."

And the funny thing was, I found myself actually believing him.

I had a hard time concentrating on my classes that day. In English I was really trying to pay attention to Mr. Cloverhill, but all I could think of was my dad's angry face and how Luke had been treated so unfairly. I wanted to believe him when he said things would work out, but I didn't want to be naïve. It was going to be practically impossible to change my dad's mind. I wondered what Dr. Sheridan would say about the whole situation. I could really use her advice on this one. *Maybe I'll call her,* I thought.

I was absently copying something from the board when a voice spoke up from the back of the classroom.

"Can I have Neesha's seat, Mr. Cloverhill? I can't see the board very well."

The voice belonged to T.J. Miller. Neesha Patel was absent that day. Normally she sat in the seat behind mine. My body tensed when Mr. Cloverhill told T.J. to move up.

The hairs on the back of my neck stood on end as T.J. slid into the seat behind me. I gripped my pen and stared at the chalkboard, the words swimming before my eyes.

"Nobody believed me about you," T.J. whispered, the sound of his voice making my heart lurch. "But they believe me now," he added softly. "Now that they've read all about you in the newspaper."

I forced myself to ignore him, and tried to focus on what Mr. Cloverhill was saying. There were only three minutes left of class. Three more minutes of torture.

"Willa Cather was a literary trailblazer on the American scene." As Mr. Cloverhill continued his lecture, I felt a finger run softly down the nape of my neck.

Startled, I dropped my pen on the floor. I was sure that every pair of eyes in the classroom was on me, and when the bell rang, I leaped to my feet and practically knocked over the girl in front of me. I raced from the room.

By the time I got to my locker, I was choking back angry tears. I wanted to stand up to T.J.—to humiliate him the way he was humiliating me. To let him know what it felt like.

But mostly I wanted to take away his power over me. I wished I didn't care what he said to me, that nothing he did could hurt me. There had to be a way to get him out of my life. I just had to find it.

# Chapter 15

"**T**urn to your right," Marlene said. She was sitting on our couch, studying me with a critical eye.

I did as she asked, the soft silky fabric of the pants swishing as I moved. Marlene had brought over four different outfits for me to try on, to see which would make the best impression at my dad's speech.

"I'm not sure. Spencer, what do you think?" she asked, looking over at my dad. He was sitting in his recliner reading *Time*.

He looked up at us and shrugged. "She looks beautiful, Mar."

Marlene frowned. "You've said that each time, Spencer."

He grinned. "Can I help it if I have a beautiful daughter?"

I didn't grin back. Nothing he said was going to make me crack a smile. And I still couldn't believe I was letting Marlene do this to me. One more stiff knee-length skirt, flowered scarf, or stupid hair accessory and I was going to scream!

I was in the middle of trying on a jacket when the phone rang. My dad picked up.

"Who's calling?" he asked. A beat. "No, she can't come to the phone. And don't call her again."

I stared at him as he clicked off. "Who was that?" I asked. "Was it Luke?"

"In case you think I wasn't serious, Maya, you are to stay away from Luke Perez," my father said, putting down his magazine and looking me square in the eye.

"I know you were serious," I said, my voice rising. "But I never thought you could be so unfair! I knew that you'd never let me go out with him. That's why I didn't tell you about it."

Dad's eyes flashed with anger. "Maya, listen to me. I expect you to tell that boy not to call this house again. If he does, I'll have to ground you for another week."

"Go ahead!" I cried. "I don't have anything to do anyway. Not the way you run my life!"

"I'm not trying to run your life." Dad's stern voice grew louder. "But I do expect you to do as you're told!"

"That's right," I shot back. "You don't want a real daughter—just a perfect little candidate's daughter.

Someone to trot out in front of the reporters when you need her—and ignore the rest of the time!"

"Maya! I'm only trying to do what's best for you. I thought you were mature enough to understand that."

"You don't know what's best for me!" I shouted. "How could you? You don't even know me! You don't know anything about me—and you don't care!"

I ran from the room, the tags on my clothes flying.

"Maya, get back here!" Dad called after me. "Maya!"

I paused at the top of the stairs. "You're not just running my life," I shouted down at him. "You're ruining it!"

I ran into my room, slamming the door shut behind me. I was not going to let my dad make me a prisoner in the castle. And how dare he talk to Luke that way?

I had to get in touch with Luke. I refused to let Dad boss me around anymore—not when he was so wrong. I went online and checked my mailbox. There were two e-mails:

> Hi, Maya,
> How are you doing? I'm not so great. I can't
> believe Alex is suddenly, completely out of my

life. Losing my boyfriend is one thing, but losing one of my closest friends. . . . How did this happen???

    Jess

 

Maya,

    Well, I just finished deleting more unopened e-mail from my "dad." I'm starting to think of him as SOS, source of spam. You'd think he'd get it by now that I don't want to correspond. Are things any better in the castle? Let me know.

    Love, Kerri

I sent a quick one back to Jessica, telling her to keep her chin up, and an even quicker one to Kerri. Suddenly an instant message popped up on the screen.

    **CoolHand: Hi Maya! Whassup? This is Luke.**

*Luke must have added me to his Buddy List!* I thought happily. I typed back:

    **Maya944: Hi! Sorry about my dad. I couldn't believe he wouldn't let me talk to you. I'm really embarrassed.**
    **CoolHand: Not your fault.**
    **Maya944: He's just so unfair!**

> **CoolHand:** Yeah. Seems that way. So what's going on?
>
> **Maya944:** Just finished a horrible makeover session with my dad and Marlene.
>
> **CoolHand:** Why? You don't need to be made over!
>
> **Maya944:** Thanks.

*He's so sweet,* I thought. Then I realized that I'd probably never see Luke outside of school ever again. I started fuming about the fight with my father. *If Dad had his way, I'd never leave my room,* I thought. *Then he could go to as many political functions as he wanted without having to worry about me having a life. Marlene's probably downstairs helping him find a padlock for my door right now!* I thrummed my fingers on my keyboard for a second. Then I typed something else:

> **Maya944:** Hey. Do you want to meet somewhere to talk?
>
> **Maya944:** Luke?
>
> **CoolHand:** Sorry, I spilled my Coke on my computer table. I don't know. I don't want your dad to get any madder than he already is. But I want to see you.
>
> **Maya944:** Can you meet me at the lake by

that World War I statue? I'll take care of my dad.
Don't worry.

I logged off and immediately changed into black
jeans, a black sweatshirt, and black Keds. If I was
going to sneak out I had to blend into the darkness.

I dabbed on some perfume and some lip gloss. I
gave myself a quick once-over in the mirror that
hung on the back of my bedroom door, feeling a tiny
rush of excitement as I fixed my hair. Then I stopped.

*What am I doing?* I wondered. I crossed the room
and sat on the edge of my bed. *I can't sneak out of my
house. What if Dad comes in to say goodnight and finds
me missing?* I shook my head. I couldn't go. I wanted
to see Luke, but who knew what my Dad would do if
he found out about it. What was I thinking?

I had to tell Luke that I changed my mind. I
glanced at my computer. E-mail wasn't good enough.
He might not read it. I had to risk using the phone. I
grabbed it off my nightstand, and dialed Luke's
number. No answer.

I sighed. Now what? I couldn't just leave Luke
waiting for me. I *had* to go.

I quickly shoved some pillows under my covers
so it looked as though I was sleeping. It probably
wouldn't work, but it was the only thing I could think
of. Then I flicked off my bedroom light, and hoped

that Dad wouldn't come into my room.

Holding my breath, I crept out of my room and down the stairs. I could hear my dad and his team talking in the living room.

"I guess that's about it," Marlene said.

"Good," I heard Dad say. "Let's wrap this up, and you can all go home."

The meeting was breaking up! Moving as silently as I could, I slipped into the ground-floor guestroom. I headed straight for the window and unlocked it. Wait—had I shut the door behind me? I turned and checked. Yes, the door was shut. I turned back to the window and slowly lifted the sash.

I swung one leg over the sill. The window had looked much bigger before I stuffed my body into its frame, I thought, trying to stay calm as my foot touched the ground. I swung my other leg out. Carefully, I pulled the window down.

I paused just outside the window, preparing to sprint across the damp grass. Suddenly a splash of light cut through the darkness, and my father stepped out onto our front steps.

I crouched low to the ground and crawled behind a shrub a few feet away. But it was too late. Dad turned in my direction.

I was caught!

# Chapter 16

**I** held my breath as my dad seemed to stare right at me. Then he switched his attention to the front door. I sighed in relief. He hadn't seen me after all.

"Spencer." Marlene stepped outside. "I left the flow charts with Peter. He's going to look at the numbers. So I'll see you tomorrow?"

My dad turned to her. "We'll have lunch," he promised. "Thanks again for all the help, Mar."

Still crouched behind the shrub, I heard every beat of my heart echo in my ears. I watched, barely breathing as Marlene and my dad talked softly for a few more minutes. Then Marlene went to her car, her heels clicking on the stone walkway. My dad waved good-bye and went back inside, shutting the door behind him as Marlene circled around the driveway and drove off.

When I was sure he was safely inside the house,

I ran to my car and slipped inside. I didn't turn on the lights until I pulled into the street.

I drove to the lake. But it wasn't like I was planning some big make-out session or anything. It was just a quiet, private place—and a place where Luke and I could talk.

I parked under a street lamp and walked over to the statue.

Luke was waiting there for me. "Hey," he said, his voice soft. "You really did it!"

I nodded. "Only because I couldn't chicken out. I tried to call you, but you were gone. And I almost got caught too. But for once I got lucky."

"*We* got lucky," Luke said. Then he frowned. "Are you going to be warm enough?"

I held up the fleece jacket that I always kept in my car. "I think so."

"Well, if you're cold, you can borrow my jacket," Luke said as walked the short distance to the lakeshore. Moonlight streaked the water, making it look dark and glossy. There were a bunch of small docks that lined the shore, with boats anchored to the posts.

We sat on a bench. Luke put his arm around my shoulders, and I rested my head against his. If I was going to get in trouble for sneaking out, I figured I'd better make it worth it.

We stayed there, nestled in each other's arms as the water gently lapped the lakeshore. It was so peaceful.

Luke smoothed back my hair. "Your dad puts a lot of pressure on you, Maya. It's like you're living under a microscope or something."

I pretended to look confused. "Campaign? Speeches? Spin doctors? I don't know what you're talking about."

Luke laughed and kissed me—and I kissed him back. We talked under the stars for an hour. About school, about our families, about our plans for the future. After T.J., it was still hard to believe that a guy could be so nice.

I never wanted our talk to end.

When I finally got back home, I practically skipped back to the house. I'd had such a great time.

The guest room window was just as I'd left it. Quietly, I raised the sash, and climbed back inside the house.

Then the Tiffany lamp clicked on. My dad stood beside it, his face twisted with anger.

I gulped. This time I wasn't so lucky.

# Chapter 17

**"Y**ou won't be needing these," my dad said, plucking the keys to my BMW from my hand. I'd never seen him so angry. "Peter will be driving you to and from school from now on." He put the keys in his pocket. "To say that I am disappointed in you would be an understatement."

"Dad, please," I begged. "Please let me explain."

"I don't want to hear it." He turned away, his shoulders slumped. "I've got to prepare for my speech tomorrow. I don't have time to hear any more stories. I've heard enough stories from you for one week."

"Hey, you," Kerri said as I slid into the seat next to her. Tuesday morning's assembly was about to begin.

"You look tired," Erin said, peering at my eyes.

"I am." I gave them the quick version of last

night's events. "I couldn't fall asleep. I just kept tossing and turning, thinking about my dad, thinking about Luke."

"I for one am impressed that you had the guts to sneak out of the house for love," Erin said. "I wish I could find love in Madison . . . are all the good guys in Seattle?"

"Not all," Kerri said, pointing to where Matt sat with his friends down front.

"What happened to Study Hall Guy?" I asked.

Erin scowled. "He stood up. Six inches shorter than me!" She shrugged. "I've got to accept it. No one here is as cool as Keith." Her eyes clouded over. "But he hasn't e-mailed me in four days. I can't figure it out."

"Too bad he can't see how many guys have been asking you out," I told her.

Erin shook her head. "I don't want to make him jealous. I just want to know what's going on in his life—if he still thinks about me as much as I think about him. This long-distance stuff is the pits."

"Why don't you call him up and ask him what his deal is?" Jessica asked. "Don't play games. It's better to be sure." Then she frowned. I followed her gaze to see Alex sitting next to Gretchen a few rows ahead of us. *Oh, no,* I thought, my heart heavy. Alex looked like he was in the middle of a story, and Gretchen was laughing, touching him on the arm and playing with her long curly hair. I looked away. Jessica stared down at her lap and began folding and unfolding the hem of her blouse.

Kerri slipped her arm around Jessica and gave her a squeeze.

Jessica's shoulders slumped. "I've been kicking myself for breaking up with him."

"Maybe there's still a chance you can get him back," I said, trying to be encouraging.

She nodded. "I wish."

We all grew quiet as Ms. Chapp, our senior class adviser, stepped up to the podium. When the assembly was over, I grabbed my books and felt a tap on my shoulder. I looked up to see Luke smiling down at me.

"Do you want to go to the game together on Friday?" he asked.

I paused—but only for a moment. "Sure," I said, feeling excited and anxious at once. My grounding would officially be over on Friday.

"Great. Meet you by the first concession stand?"

I nodded. "Okay."

Luke gave me a curious look as we filed out of the auditorium. "About Friday. You're not going to tell your dad that you're going to the game with me, are you?"

"I don't know," I answered. "I want to be

completely honest with him. But I kind of doubt that we're going to get to that point by this Friday."

The sun was beating down when I stepped onto the field for hockey practice that afternoon. I slipped off my navy Adidas jacket. Although I wasn't warmed up yet, I knew I'd be sweaty within minutes. Unless it was freezing out, I always wore running shorts and a sweatshirt for practice. I stood in front of the bench, shielding my eyes from the sun, trying to make out who was on the grass.

"Guess who?" a male voice said from behind me. An arm slipped around my waist.

I spun around. T.J. grinned down at me. Two of his friends were standing behind him. "I've been missing you," he said in a fake-romantic voice. His friends stood a few feet behind him, laughing.

A rush of anger swept through me. "Get away from me!" I screamed, shoving him as hard as I could. From the look on his face I knew I'd startled him. I'd startled myself too. But I was too busy being angry to check myself.

"Don't you ever put your hands on me again," I yelled, whacking him in the shin with my field hockey stick. The wood cracked against his leg.

T.J. yelped with pain. "Ouch! What are you doing?"

His friends started laughing. "You're right," one of them said. "She's a wild one!"

I ignored the comment, and clenched my stick, ready to bash T.J.'s face in if he said another word to me.

T.J. held up his hands and moved back, limping slightly. I watched, gritting my teeth, as they sauntered off. My whole body was shaking as I picked up my water bottle and took a swig. I couldn't believe that I'd actually hit him!

Two of my teammates, Ari Wiley and Melissa Klein, came jogging over.

"Are you okay?" Ari asked me hesitantly, her brown eyes wide.

I nodded, my throat still dry. "I'm okay. Thanks."

"What's the deal between you and T.J.?" Melissa asked warily.

I'd always thought Melissa was nice. "He's just a jerk who won't leave me alone," I told her, putting down the bottle. Suddenly I felt drained. "Hey, guys, do you think you could tell Coach Dobson that I'm going to skip practice? I can't deal with being here right now." All I wanted to do was to go home and curl up in my bed, maybe write in my journal.

Just then I saw Peter's car pulling up alongside the school. He must have forgotten I had practice after school—but lucky for me he had. "Just a minute!" I yelled, waving at him. I ran back inside the school and changed into my jeans and sweater, stuffing my practice clothes in my duffel bag. Then I rushed out to the car.

"Hi," I said, dropping into the passenger seat. "Boy, am I glad to see you."

"Likewise," he said, giving me a sidelong glance. I zoned out, closing my eyes. But when I opened them a few minutes later, we were not on the road that led to the castle.

"Where are we going?" I asked, confused.

Peter looked at me as if I had two heads. "To the Hewlett Hotel. To hear your father announce his candidacy, remember?"

My heart stopped. "No. I can't!" I cried, clutching the door handle. "Peter! Stop the car!"

# Chapter 18

**P**eter glanced at me, then stared at the road. I could tell he thought I'd lost my mind. "Maya, I can't stop the car. We'll be late for your dad's speech."

"You don't understand," I told him, panicking. "I'm supposed to wear this special outfit Marlene got me from Neiman Marcus." I looked down at my jeans and sneakers. "I can't go like this! My dad's already angry with me."

With everything that had been going on lately, I'd forgotten about Dad's announcement.

Peter raised a blond eyebrow.

"The outfit's hanging in my closet," I pleaded, gripping the leather seat. "If we go back to the house, I promise I'll be fast."

Peter shook his head. "There's no time. We're already fifteen minutes behind schedule. If you think your dad's angry with you now, wait and see what happens if you miss this speech."

In my father's world, fifteen minutes behind schedule was the equivalent of a tornado touching down in Kansas. I fell back against the cool leather, knowing Peter was right.

Twenty minutes later Peter escorted me into the Hewlett Hotel's Grand Ballroom. Cavanaugh-Greer banners hung from every wall. Henry Cavanaugh, the candidate for governor, was onstage talking to the crowd. My Dad was standing behind him. I'd caught the last few minutes of Cavanaugh's speech when Marlene marched up to us.

"You've got to be kidding," she said, her glare sweeping me from head to toe. "After all the time, effort, and money we spent selecting an outfit, you show up looking like that? Are you *trying* to embarrass your father?"

I felt like the worst daughter in the world.

"Look," Peter said in his best peace-keeping voice, "there's nothing either one of you can do about it now. Maya's here for her dad. That's what counts. The crowd will focus on Spencer, not on his daughter's wardrobe." He gently steered me away from Marlene. "There's a group of supporters over here who would love to meet you, Maya," he said. "They have kids in high school too."

I fixed a smile on my face and walked over to a group of women who were all wearing pastel business suits and pearl necklaces. Fortunately, while we were riding to the hotel, Peter had briefed me, telling me what to expect and when to expect it. He'd also drilled me on my father's platform—improving child care and funding for schools, making Wisconsin a leader in our nation's family resource and support programs, and his top priority: reducing the state deficit. And he'd run down a list of people that if I could, it would behoove (his word, not mine) me to talk to. That list included these women.

"This is Maya Greer, Spencer's daughter," he told them. "She's a senior at South Central."

A woman with platinum blond hair smiled at me. "Tell me, Maya," she said, "what do you think the important issues for teenagers are?"

*Feeling like your parents really listen to you, having the freedom to date anybody you want,* I wanted to answer, but I smiled and said, "I think getting more funding for the schools would have a huge impact." And then I managed to say all the right things that Peter and Marlene had been coaching me on.

An hour later I'd given so many rehearsed answers, I could barely remember what I'd said. I just hoped some of it made sense. The whole time I kept catching glimpses of my dad. He was listening to people, laughing, clearly charming them.

"How's it going?" Peter came to check on me.

"My head is spinning," I confessed. "But my father really knows how to work the crowd," I said with grudging admiration as we looked over at him. He stood tall beneath a banner that read "Vote Cavanaugh/Greer—Fighters for Wisconsin Families!"

A large, tanned man at the front of the room was finishing what seemed like a ten-minute introduction. "I can't think of anyone who could fill the role of lieutenant governor more ably than Spencer Greer. Nationally recognized as a strong advocate for improving life in America, Spencer Greer is here today to tell you his vision for our state and to officially announce his run. Ladies and gentlemen, Spencer Greer!"

I watched as my father glad-handed his way through the crowd and jogged up to the podium. He looked neat and trim in a gray suit and white shirt. I did a double-take at his tie: little boys and girls holding hands on a green background. I had given it to him years ago. I couldn't believe he still owned it, let alone that he had chosen to wear it to such an important event.

My father began his speech and it was electrifying. Everyone in the room stopped what they were doing to listen. He presented his agenda in a way that not only made you believe in what he was saying, but made you believe in him. He was articulate, funny, and sincere. And when he got a thunderous round of applause at the end of his speech, I was clapping as loudly as everyone in the room.

"There are a lot of people I'd like to thank," my father said, smiling and gesturing to people in the crowd. "A lot of unsung heroes. Marlene Carroll, publicity coordinator for Children First, the well-regarded nonprofit agency." Marlene waved from the sidelines. "We're so grateful that she's donating her expertise to our campaign." He went on to list Peter and the rest of his staff. And then, his voice tender and caring, he said, "I've got a beautiful daughter here who deserves a lot of thanks. Maya, give us a wave."

I did as he asked, and for a moment, our eyes met. It was like old times, my dad beaming proudly at me. I looked at him and it was as if all my anger of the past few days fizzled away. *I* was so proud of *him*. For living his dream, for going after what he wanted, and for doing the best job he could without my mom to support him.

As the applause died down and the crowd began to mill around once more, I headed toward my dad. I was about three feet away when one of his staffers cut in between us, whispering something in my father's ear. I was sure that meant my father wouldn't have time for me, but he waved me over.

"That was an awesome speech!" I told him.

"Maya." My dad gave me a hug. "Peter told me what a good job you've been doing here!"

I was really glad he was pleased with me. But I knew we still had to straighten things out. "Listen, Dad, we need to talk later," I said, pulling away. "It's really important."

My dad nodded but I wasn't sure he heard me. "Peter?" he called distractedly as Peter hurried to join us. "Make sure Maya gets home safely." He turned back to me. "There's someone here I've got to speak to," he said, "but we'll talk tomorrow." He flashed me a smile. "Thanks for your help, honey. I'm glad you came around. See, your dad really does know what's best for you."

I lowered my head, disappointed. Talk later? *Yeah, right,* I thought, turning away.

I told Peter I'd meet him at the car, and melted back into the crowd. I forced myself to smile as I made my way out to the parking lot. But inside I felt hollow. Okay, so I did what my dad needed. Now I needed him to make an effort for me.

In the passenger seat of the car, I immediately took out my journal and started putting down my thoughts.

"What are you writing?" Peter asked as he slipped into the driver's seat.

I stared down at the open journal in my lap. Most

people don't carry their journals with them, but I liked the freedom of being able to write any at time, in any place. Plus the idea of leaving it at home made me nervous. I couldn't be sure my father wouldn't find it.

"Nothing important," I answered. It was hard to write while the car was moving. But I just had to get my thoughts down on paper.

Dad and me . . .

In five years our relationship will be like . . . (fill in the blank). Don't know. Don't care. Scratch that. I care, but I still don't know the answer.

What DO I know? Dad's a hard worker. But at least when Mom was alive he used to take time out for us. Like we always, ALWAYS used to have dinner together. Our family time, Dad used to call it. The only time we were all together in one room.

He'd always start by asking me about whatever mini-crisis I was involved in that day. Sometimes he'd share stories about when he first met Mom. I can't believe he was afraid to ask her to dance because she was so beautiful. Good thing Mom asked HIM.

Mom would talk about her life growing up in Argentina. About all my aunts and uncles who are still over there. She'd show me pictures of the huge parties Nanna and Grandpa would throw for no reason at all. Dancing, great food, everyone cheering and singing. Dad would laugh about how my uncles teased him every time they'd visit.

He thought it was important for me to know my family in Argentina. "Maya, they're a big part of your life," he'd say. It's funny, at the time I couldn't wait to leave the table. I was sick of Dad's old stories. But now I'd give anything just to share a meal with him.

Now there's all this stuff about me that Dad doesn't know. But how can I tell him when he's not really here for me? Okay, well sure, he's been here, but not emotionally. Not where I can talk to him about things that matter. And what I realized today is that it's only going to get worse as this election heats up. He's going to be even busier, have even more people needing him. He's going to have less and less time for me. Will he and I even know each other by the time the election is over?

I stared out at the passing scenery, my gaze lingering on a woman and her small daughter crossing the street. They were holding hands. I glanced at my journal and wrote one last thing:

You know, little kids aren't the only ones who need their parents.

# Chapter 19

**"I** played the perfect daughter role so well, I should be up for an Academy Award," I told Dr. Sheridan, only half kidding. It was Wednesday afternoon, my therapy appointment, and I was telling her about my dad's formal announcement at the Hewlett.

"Maya, do you really think your father wants you to be someone you're not?" Dr. Sheridan asked.

"I don't know," I said quietly. "Lately I see so little of him, I feel like I barely know him."

She tapped her pencil on her notepad. "What would make your life perfect?" she asked me. "If you could have three wishes, what would they be?"

I thought for a moment. "I guess if T.J. would leave me alone, if my mom was alive, and if my dad would really listen to me," I said.

"Well, we can't bring back your mother. But we can work on the other two issues." She looked at me.

"Why do you think T.J. acts like he does?" she asked.

I shrugged. "He's a jerk."

Now Dr. Sheridan shrugged. "Maybe. But do you think T.J. is a happy person?"

"I don't know. I never thought about it."

"People who pick on or abuse others usually aren't very happy. They try to make others feel powerless before someone else can do that very thing to them. Usually it's because they feel powerless themselves."

Did T.J. feel powerless? It was hard to imagine. He sure was big and strong, a jock on the basketball team, and part of the really popular crowd. He didn't seem powerless.

"I'm talking about inner power," Dr. Sheridan went on. "I suspect T.J. isn't nearly as confident as he looks."

"You mean he's afraid people won't like him?"

"In a way," Dr. Sheridan said. "Maya, I know he's scary, and you should be careful not to find yourself alone with him again. But at the same time, you can't let him drive you into hiding. If he sees how strong you can be, that he can't intimidate you, he might stop trying. I think he gets satisfaction out of seeing how much of an effect he has on you. He wants to get a reaction from you, good or bad."

Wednesday afternoon

Dr. Sheridan really made me think today. We talked about T.J. She said the way I react to him encourages him. I can't let him ruin my life—but I still don't know exactly how I'm going to do that.

Now that I think of it, I'm kind of embarrassed that I hit him with my hockey stick. I'm still letting him get to me and it didn't make me feel any better.

We talked about Dad too. I told her he's just a workaholic, but Dr. Sheridan wasn't so sure. I mean, she didn't argue, but she asked a lot of questions, like "Was he always this way?" or "Does he love his work?" or "Why do you think he never talks about your mother?" I couldn't give her answers to these questions, but now I'm starting to think that maybe Dad hasn't been handling the stress in his life as well as he wants me to believe. Maybe Dad uses his work as an escape from things he doesn't want to think about—like Mom. I think it's up to me to bring up the subject. If I don't, maybe it's like I'm allowing Dad not to face things. I mean, Mom's gone, and life's never going to be the same, but we have to go on.

The more I think about it, the more I think I've got to be the one who makes things change—I can't just keep reacting to everything around me.

Okay, enough. I've got a ton of math homework.

• • •

"They don't call these nosebleed seats for nothing," Luke complained as he, Erin, Jessica, and I stomped up the packed bleachers on South Central's football field. It was Friday night, our big game against the Dunbar Dragons, and all the good seats were already taken. It was also my first day free from being grounded. Jessica and Erin and I had all planned on going to the game together, and they'd been cool about it when I'd asked if it was okay if Luke came too.

"It's my fault," I explained to Luke. "My dad put Jessica and Erin through the third degree about where we were going tonight—that's why we're half an hour late."

"Could have been worse," Jessica said. "For a moment there, I thought your dad was going to come with us."

"My father loves football," I explained to Luke.

"I think those seats are fine," Erin said, pointing to an empty row above us. "How much of the game are we really going to watch anyway?"

Luke laughed. "You should probably be tried for homecoming-queen heresy."

We inched our way up to the empty bleacher, balancing onion rings, sodas, Gummi Bears, pom-poms, whistles, and a hand-lettered sign that said, MATT FOWLER ROCKS! Kerri had given us the sign and made us promise to hold it up.

"Keith finally returned my e-mail," Erin said, sitting down beside Jessica.

"What took him so long?" Jessica asked.

"Keith is this guy Erin met in Seattle," I whispered to Luke.

"He's taking really tough classes this year—AP English, calculus, and physics. He's been really busy," Erin explained.

"Still," Jessica said. "I mean, I'm busy like that too, but I make time to stay in touch with my friends."

"He's in a lot of clubs at school too," Erin said a little defensively.

Privately I agreed with Jessica. But then, what did I know about guys? Maybe Keith really was too busy to e-mail.

I popped a Gummi Bear into my mouth and decided to change the subject. "No way am I holding this sign," I said, handing it to Luke. "I'd feel like a moron!"

"Oh yeah?" Luke began waving it up and down. "Waving this sign and acting like a moron is the only way you're going to keep warm up here."

Jessica reached over and tugged on his sleeve. "You mean you're not going to give Maya your jacket?"

"Jess!" I hissed, mortified.

"No way, man," Luke said, grinning. "Maya's got to get up and show her school spirit just like the rest of us." Then he leaned close to me and whispered, "The jacket's yours if you want it."

Luke looked really cute in his faded jeans with the little hole at the left knee. I'd noticed a lot of girls checking him out. Sometimes I had to pinch myself to believe that Luke was really with me.

The air was cold and crisp—a perfect night for Wisconsin football. We watched as the Lions jogged onto the field and the cheerleaders went wild. Kerri was jumping around, waving her pom-poms, and although I knew she couldn't see us, I waved at her.

"They're here," Jessica whispered to me.

I'd spotted Alex sitting with Gretchen and a bunch of her friends when we'd arrived, but I wasn't about to point them out to Jess. "Try to ignore them," I said, though I knew I'd have a hard time doing that if I were her.

After the game, we all went out for pizza to celebrate our win.

"Weren't the Lions awesome?" Kerri asked, beaming at Matt. "I screamed so much I'm hoarse."

"You were great, man," Luke said, high-fiving Matt. "From the looks of tonight, we've got the state championships locked up." He and Matt knew each other from school—they were in the same study hall. They'd never really talked before, but they had hit it off immediately.

I was having fun. A lot of fun. But we'd had to wait in line to get seats at Pizza Pi, and now it was nearly ten thirty. My dad's eleven P.M. curfew was closing in—and I knew Dad would be counting every minute. I already felt guilty for seeing Luke behind his back. I couldn't risk breaking curfew. Things were bad enough between us as it was.

Just as our pizza arrived, I whispered to Luke, "Would you mind if we left? I've got to be home by eleven, and—"

"Sure, whatever you want," Luke said. "I don't need any more trouble with the future lieutenant governor of Wisconsin."

"You're going to leave me with these three?" Matt joked, looking from Kerri to Jessica to Erin.

"Yeah, you're really suffering," Erin shot back, helping herself to a cheesy slice.

"We'll miss you, Maya," Kerri said.

"Call and let me know what time you want me to pick you up tomorrow," Jessica added. We were going bowling the next night.

Luke and I gathered our things and walked past the busy take-out counter toward the door.

"Thanks," I said to him. "I really appreciate you

underst—" I broke off as I bumped into a woman at the take-out counter. "Sorry," I started, "I—"

The woman turned around. It was Marlene Carroll. Her daughter, Amanda, was standing right next to her.

"Maya!" Marlene said. "What a coincidence meeting you here!"

*Oh, no,* I thought. *Of all the pizza places in Madison, why did she have to show up at this one?*

"Maya, this is my daughter, Amanda," Marlene said.

"She knows, Mom," Amanda said. "We've seen each other around school."

"And you are?" Marlene asked Luke.

"Luke Perez," he said, extending his hand—and sealing my fate. Marlene was going to tell my father. I just knew she was going to tell him.

# *Chapter 20*

**"H**ere's your pie." The guy behind the take-out counter handed Amanda a large pizza box.

Marlene and I stared at each other for what seemed like an endless moment. Then Marlene did something that I never in a million years would have expected. She put her finger to her lips in a "Shhh" sign. I stared in amazement as she and Amanda walked out.

"What was *that* all about?" Luke asked.

"Good question." I hung back in the restaurant to make sure they were gone before we went outside.

"That woman looked familiar," Luke said. "Didn't I see her on TV when your dad made his big campaign announcement?"

"Yeah, she works with my dad."

Luke grabbed my arm. "Will she tell him about us?"

"I don't think so. I think that's what she meant

when she put her finger to her lips."

But I wasn't sure. I'd seen how Marlene operated. Maybe she wouldn't tell, but she was definitely going to expect something from me. "There's no way she's letting me slide. I'll owe her big now."

*I can't sneak around like this,* I thought the next morning. *I'll tell Dad about Luke and get it out in the open, so at least I won't have to feel guilty about it. And that way, Marlene won't have any dirt on me.*

But when I got down to the kitchen, my dad, Peter, Marlene, and a couple of other staffers were in the middle of a Saturday morning pancake powwow. *Ah, one big happy political family,* I thought, realizing there was no way I could talk to Dad now.

I decided to grab a bowl of cereal and get out of there. My day was all mapped out. I had to work on a paper for history class and study for a physics test. And then in the evening, bowling with Jessica. Kerri and Matt had a date, and Erin had scheduled a phone call with Keith, so it would just be the two of us.

I was reaching for the milk when Dad interrupted his meeting to talk to me. "I'm having dinner tonight with some of the Milwaukee contingent," he said. "I'm going to spend the night at Senator Boxell's house—I won't be back until tomorrow morning." He put down his coffee mug. "The security system will be on, and I'll leave the numbers where I can be reached. And you have my cell phone number."

"Okay," I said. "Jessica and I planned to go bowling tonight, if that's okay."

He nodded. "Fine. Maybe she could spend the night with you?"

I shrugged. "Maybe."

My dad and his staff continued their conversation. I opened the dishwasher in search of a clean spoon. Marlene got up from the table and stood beside me at the counter.

"Maya, I wanted to . . . to apologize for being so harsh lately," she said quietly. "It's just that the campaign is so important right now . . . this is the crucial make-or-break stage," she explained, distractedly running her fingers through her frizzy hair.

"Well, thanks," I said awkwardly. "I, um, know you want what's best for my dad."

She smiled as she refilled her coffee mug. "Yes, I do."

I took a deep breath. "And thanks for not ratting on me," I added, wondering if she was going to ask me to do a favor for her.

Instead she patted me gently on the shoulder.

"You looked like you were having a great time," she said, her eyes uncharacteristically warm. "I hope things work out."

As she walked back to join the men at the table, it struck me that Marlene Carroll might have a heart after all.

"I love these things!" Jessica stuck out her white-and-blue bowling shoe–clad feet, wiggling them happily. It was Saturday Night Madness at Ten Pin Alley, and Jessica and I had just taken a lane. "Why don't we ever wear them out in the real world?"

I giggled. "Nothing from the bowling alley world must enter the real world," I said mock-seriously. "If you allow bowling shoes out onto the street, then you'll want to take bowling balls too. The next thing you know, people will be knocking each other down on the sidewalk like tenpins."

Jessica rolled her eyes. "Sometimes you're really sick, Maya," she said, but she seemed distracted. I caught her starting to glance to the left, then stopping herself. She forced herself to stare at the scoreboard projected over our heads.

She was struggling not to look at the guys bowling a few lanes over from us, and I knew why. One of them was Alex McKay. Alex had waved to us when we walked in, and ignored us ever since.

"Check this out," Jessica said, jumping up and grabbing her ball. With a flourish, she stepped forward and let the ball glide from her hand. It rolled down the lane, cracking the pins and sending them scattering.

"Steee-rike!" I cried.

Jess whooped, high-fiving me. A few people in the lane next to us glanced over, amused. But not Alex.

"Why don't you go and talk to him?" I asked. "Enough torture."

"I don't know if I can," Jessica said, looking miserable. She covered her face with her hands.

"If anyone could walk over there, it's you, Jess. You're one of the bravest people I know."

She peeked through her fingers. "You think so?"

"I really do," I said. "Look." I reached into my bag and pulled out my journal, flipped to a page I'd written last week, and read, "I wish I had Jessica's confidence. She always says what's on her mind. But me? Instead of telling my dad how I feel I just end up writing everything in this journal." I handed the book to Jessica. "See?"

"You think I'm confident?" she said, turning the pages. "I always thought *you* were. And look! You've written so much."

"Dr. Sheridan asked me to. It's been good to have

a place where I can say anything. But I wish I could tell my dad this stuff to his face instead of writing it here," I told her. "It's kind of like a letter that I'll never mail."

"Do you mind if I read a page?" Jessica asked.

"Go ahead. You've heard it all before, anyway."

A few minutes later Jessica looked up at me. "This is really good, Maya."

"Thanks," I said, flattered that someone who wrote as well as Jessica did thought what I wrote was okay.

Jessica bopped me on the head with my journal. "No, I mean *really* good. You should definitely try to get this published. It's powerful. You really articulate what you went through . . . what you're going through now."

"I don't think so," I said, kind of embarrassed. "That's nice of you to say, though." But I couldn't even consider it. This was way too private for anyone except my friends to see.

As Jessica tried to convince me, I snuck a glance at Alex. He was sitting on the bench, stretching his arms over his head.

"Jess, why don't you tell Alex what *you're* going through? How *you're* feeling."

Jessica shook her head. "I can't."

"You can!" I insisted. "Besides, Gretchen isn't

here. Who knows when you'll have an opportunity like this again?"

Jessica's dark eyes flashed. "Okay," she said suddenly. "Okay, I'll do it." She swallowed. "But I've got to do it now, before I chicken out."

"You'll be fine," I assured her as she stood up. "It's just Alex."

"Right. It's just Alex," she repeated as she started toward his lane.

I wanted to watch, but I didn't want to make her nervous. Instead I slipped into the seat in front of the computer scoreboard to see how we were doing.

I felt a tap on my shoulder.

"Hey, Maya." Amanda Carroll stood behind me, smiling. She was with a couple of other girls I recognized from school. "Are you by yourself?"

"No, I'm with my friend Jessica," I replied, nodding toward Alex's lane. "She's over there."

Amanda introduced me to her friends, Gina and Stephanie. "It's so funny, running into you two nights in a row!" Amanda said. "I guess you're not grounded anymore."

How did she know I'd been grounded? Marlene must have told her. "No, I'm not grounded," I confirmed.

"Isn't that great about our parents?" Amanda asked me.

I shrugged. "Yeah, they make a good team."

Amanda nodded. "My mom hasn't dated anyone in a long time. It took me a little while to get used to it, but now I think they look pretty cute together—for an old couple, I mean."

I stared at Amanda. I didn't know what to say.

"I think it's great that they're dating. Don't you?"

I felt the color drain from my face.

My dad was *dating*? Dating *Marlene*? It felt like the air was being squeezed out of my chest.

"Oh. Uh . . . yeah, sure," I finally managed. "I think it's just terrific."

# Chapter 21

I watched as Amanda and her friends walked away, trying to make sense of what she'd just told me.

"So I did it," Jessica said excitedly, rejoining me a minute later. She squeezed my hand. "Alex and I had a really good talk. For the first time in weeks I felt this great vibe. . . ." She broke off. "Maya? Is something wrong?" Her dark eyes darted around. "Is T.J. here?"

"No. No, it's nothing like that," I said slowly. I looked at Jessica. "I just found out that my dad is seeing Marlene Carroll."

"His PR person?" Jessica gasped. "But how—"

"Marlene's daughter, Amanda, is here with her friends. She just told me." I let out a weak laugh. "She obviously had no clue that I didn't know."

"Maybe you misunderstood her," Jessica said cautiously.

I shook my head. "No. No, Jess. My dad and Marlene . . . my dad and Marlene Carroll are a couple."

After that I didn't feel much like bowling anymore. Jessica dropped me off at the castle, and I sat on the couch in our family room, aimlessly channel surfing and trying to make sense of the whole thing.

How could my father have started dating without even mentioning it to me? When did he even have time to date?

The more I thought about it, the more I stopped feeling so shocked, and started feeling angry.

How could he be dating? Here I was, worried sick about seeing Luke behind his back, and all along he'd been seeing Marlene behind my back. So much for the great honesty pact!

How could I have been so blind that I totally missed the romance going on between them? The way my father called her "Mar." How she was so overconcerned with every little detail pertaining to him. I thought back to all the times Marlene had been in our home. All the breakfasts and dinners, all the late-night meetings. The "political" trips they'd gone on together.

*He's been lying to me the whole time!* I thought.

Right now I was really glad he was at a fund-raising event, because I didn't think I could deal with seeing him.

But maybe he wasn't at a fund-raising event. Maybe he had lied about that too. Maybe he was on a date with Marlene!

I walked down the hallway to the kitchen, my heels clacking on the marble floor. I'd made sure to turn on all the downstairs lights when Jessica had dropped me off so I wouldn't be scared, but suddenly I didn't want to be alone.

I picked up the kitchen phone and punched in Luke's number. He answered on the second ring.

"Luke?" I said, suddenly shy. I'd never called him before.

"Yes?"

"Um, it's Maya," I said.

"Hey, Maya." He sounded happy to hear my voice. "What's up?"

I swallowed. "Oh, well, Jessica just dropped me off—we went bowling at Ten Pin Alley."

"I'm watching TV with my dad," he said. "Why'd you call it quits so early on a Saturday night?"

I blinked back tears. "I . . . I didn't feel like staying, I guess." Then I blurted out what Amanda had told me at the bowling alley.

"Are you sure she had her facts straight?" Luke asked.

There was no doubt in my mind. Everything about it made sense. "I'm sure, Luke. My dad and Marlene are a couple." I couldn't hold it back any longer. I started to cry.

Luke waited a few seconds. "Do you want me to come over?"

"Would you mind?" I asked gratefully. The thought of Luke being here already made me feel better.

"I'll be there in a half hour," he promised.

"My mom hasn't even been gone for two years. How can he think about being with someone else?" I sobbed. Luke and I were in the family room, curled up together on a couch.

Luke shook his head. "Everyone's different, Maya. This doesn't mean he's forgotten your mom." Luke's dark hair was tousled and his cheeks were flushed because he'd hurried to get here.

I wiped my eyes and pointed to the portrait of my mom that hung above the fireplace. "She had this deep laugh . . . I loved trying to make her laugh." I wrapped my arms around a chenille pillow. "She wasn't the type of person to go around smiling all the time, but when she did, you knew it was for real, that her face always reflected how she felt inside."

"You must miss her a lot," Luke said.

I nodded, sniffling. "She always tried to make me feel special. I remember one time I'd had this really bad day at school and when I came home, she was in the middle of organizing her slides. One look at my face and she dropped everything to listen to me, to try to cheer me up. It was only after I was supposed to have gone to bed that I heard her tell my dad she was going to have to postpone the lecture she'd been planning because her materials weren't ready. But she never put me off for something like that. Never."

"My mom was like that too," Luke said. "She worked a lot of late hours—she worked as a nurse until a few months before she died—but she always put me first. Even though she wasn't always there when I got home, she'd leave me little notes and stuff. Like 'Do your homework!' or 'Make your bed!' Stuff like that."

I felt so dumb then. Here I was crying on Luke's shoulder about my mom, when he had gone through the same thing.

"It's just that I never saw this coming in a million years," I said. "Why didn't he tell me the truth, Luke? We promised each other we'd be honest. We even made a pact."

Luke wrapped an arm around me, pulling me close. "I don't want to be the bad guy here, Maya, but you haven't exactly been honest with him either."

"That's because I knew how he'd react!" I said.

"Well, maybe that's why your dad never told you about Marlene," Luke said, wiping a fresh tear away from my blotchy cheek.

I shrugged, dejected. Maybe my father had been afraid to tell me. But that still didn't excuse his behavior. This was a big deal. This was something he should have sat down and told me.

"You just need to get used to the idea," Luke leaned over and started to kiss me. I kissed him back, melting into his arms. All my problems, the room around us, the whole world seemed to fade away until there was nothing left but Luke and me.

"What is going on?" my father's voice thundered.

Startled, I opened my eyes and jumped off the couch, surprised. Dad was supposed to be in Milwaukee tonight.

My father was red-faced, glaring at Luke. "Well, Maya?"

"Dad," I said quickly. "I can explain!"

# Chapter 22

"**D**ad, it's not what it looks like," I said.

"Then why don't you tell me what it is." My dad's voice had become frighteningly calm. I knew he was furious.

Luke bolted up, looking alarmed. His hair was sticking up in little clumps, and his sweater was all rumpled.

"Leave." My father wouldn't even look at him.

Luke did as my father said.

"I don't understand you anymore," my dad barked at me. He began to pace back and forth. "You've completely betrayed my trust."

"Wait a minute, Dad." I was getting angry too. After all, I wasn't the only one who'd been less than honest.

But he didn't stop. "You're sixteen, Maya. I leave you alone for one night and come back to find you here with a boy? It's a good thing I decided to come home."

"Luke is my friend," I said hotly. "I know you think just because you told me not to see him that I wouldn't, but you can't tell me how to live my life. You're never around anyway!"

My father's expression grew even angrier, if that was possible. "You gave me your word you would be honest, Maya."

"And you gave me yours," I shot back. "Tell me, Dad, how was Senator Boxell? Or were you with Marlene?" I shrugged. "I mean, she is your girlfriend, right?"

"Maya." For once my in-control father looked stunned.

I stared at him, challenging him.

"This isn't how I wanted—"

"To tell me?" I finished. "No, apparently you didn't want to tell me at all. I had to find out from Amanda. Apparently Marlene talks to her daughter about things that matter. But I wouldn't know what that's like."

"Maya, this isn't how I meant for you to find out," my dad said quietly. "I should have told you sooner. I'm sorry."

"Our honesty pact was a total failure," I said.

"It certainly looks that way," my father agreed sadly. He suddenly looked tired. He sat down on the ottoman.

"I wish I could be here more for you," he said. "I want to know about your life, about what's important to you. But how do you expect that to happen with the way you've been acting?"

I'm not sure if what I did next came out of anger or desperation or both. But I strode over to the foyer where I'd dumped my backpack after bowling. Reaching inside, I pulled out my journal and walked back into the room.

"You want to know about my life? Well, here it is," I said, handing him my journal.

Never in a million years would I have imagined I'd do such a thing. But I was beyond feeling embarrassed now. What I had written was the truth. So he wanted to know about me? Well, he was about to find out. No more secrets.

# Chapter 23

"**W**hen you're a senior in high school." I'd read and reread the first line of the essay I'd written the night before. It was Monday morning, and I'd been standing outside the *Spectrum* office for the past five minutes, trying to work up the courage to go inside. *And you'd better hurry!* I scolded myself. The substitute teacher would wonder where I had disappeared with my hall pass, and if I didn't move it, the bell would ring, and Alex would be heading off to his next class, and it would be too late.

Taking a deep breath, I pushed open the old wooden door. Alex sat at one of the computer terminals, typing away.

"Greetings," he said, looking up from the keyboard and giving me a wave. "What's up?"

I smiled, suddenly shy. "Hi, Alex." I'd always liked Alex, and every time I saw him I was sorry all over again that he and Jessica had broken up. He'd always been really nice to all of us. He'd become our friend too. I was glad that he was still a reporter for the school paper—even after he'd become editor-in-chief of the yearbook. It made what I was about to do much easier.

I held out the sheets of paper I'd been holding in my hand. They were pretty wrinkled now. "I, um, I know you're always looking for editorial pieces, and I've written something that you might, uh, want to look at."

His eyes widened. "Sure. I'd love to read it."

I hesitated, then gave it to him, knowing that once I did, I could never take my words back.

But I was okay with that.

Right after the big scene with my dad last night, I'd called Luke. Finally having our relationship out in the open had lifted a huge weight from my shoulders. Sneaking around—that wasn't me. Lying and playing games—that wasn't me either. I'd never gone behind my father's back, and I decided I never would again. I might make decisions my father didn't approve of—but at least I wanted to give him the opportunity to tell me so.

I'd called Kerri too. She picked me up and took me to her house. I'd needed to get away while Dad went through my journal, and he'd said it was okay for me to sleep over. I guess he understood how awkward I felt about him reading my personal thoughts.

Sunday evening, when I'd finally gone home, I found a note on my dresser.

*Maya—*

*I had to go to a fund-raiser tonight, but honey, we really need to talk—especially about T.J. I'm so sorry that I haven't been here for you. Call me on my cell when you get home.*

*I love you.*

*Dad*

I'd called Dad to tell him I was okay, and that we'd have a long talk tomorrow. After that I tried to sleep, but I couldn't. My mind was racing with all sorts of thoughts and emotions. I was so used to having my journal to write in that not having it made me feel lost.

So I got out some paper and began writing, trying to sort it all out. And when I read what I had written, I realized it was really good. I wanted other people to read it. This was the best way to show everyone—most important myself—that T.J. couldn't hurt me anymore. And that I had the strength to overcome the bad things that may happen in life.

But still, I was feeling kind of funny as I watched

Alex scan my words. It's one thing to write your innermost thoughts down on paper, but it's another to watch someone else read them.

Alex suddenly looked up. "This is terrific, Maya." He jumped to his feet. "I want to go catch Frank and see if we can still make the print run for tomorrow's paper."

I blinked, not expecting things to happen so fast. "You really want to publish it?"

"You sound surprised," Alex said, shaking his head. "You have no idea how hard it is to find good pieces. You really have talent, Maya. And guts.

"You don't have to sign your name if you don't want to," he went on. "That's totally fine."

I nodded. "Okay. Thanks."

Alex smiled and headed out of the room.

*After all the stuff you've been through, you're too chicken to sign your name?* Suddenly it hit me. Turning in an anonymous piece was lame. What would that say about me? That I was still scared? That I was still afraid to be honest?

"Hey, Alex!" I yelled, jogging after him. "Wait up!"

That day everyone but Jessica was at lunch—she was at the university, taking her classes.

"I finally got in all my paperwork to the

University of Miami for early admission," Kerri announced. She pretended to bite her nails. "Now the wait begins."

"I can't believe that you would actually apply to a school so far away from here," I said, twirling a French fry.

"Yeah," Erin chimed in. "Isn't that against the law for best friends?"

Kerri took a bite of her grilled cheese sandwich. "I know, I know. It's just that Miami's got a great physical therapy program." She grinned. "And the fact that it's right by the beach doesn't hurt either!"

"Don't worry, we'll be visiting," I said, smiling.

"I'm still waiting for that design school in Seattle to send me a catalog," Erin griped. She reached under the table and pulled out a large envelope from her fake leopard fur tote bag. "But I did get something really cool via snail-mail."

"A letter from Keith?" Kerri asked.

Erin laughed. "No, Keith's a total techie. He probably doesn't even realize there is another way to write besides e-mail. But we did have a great talk on Saturday." She frowned. "I just wish we could have talked longer. His parents made him get off after thirty minutes." She laid a thick cream-colored envelope on the table. "But guess what? Aunt Joyce wants me to be her maid of honor! She sent me a ton of fabric swatches so I can pick out the color of my dress."

"Wow!" I exclaimed.

"Cool!" Kerri's eyes were dreamy. "You'll have so much fun. You'll get to wear a gorgeous gown, have your hair done, get a French manicure . . ."

"And you'll get to see Keith," I added.

Erin licked her lips. "I know. I'm kind of nervous about that. I haven't seen him in so long! What if he's different now? What if he thinks I'm different? What if he doesn't like me anymore?"

"Are you kidding?" I said. "How could he not like the homecoming queen?"

"And you'll look even more fabulous than usual," Kerri put in. "You'll be the total bridal babe!"

"I hope so," Erin said. "I really like him. I've tried dating other guys, but . . . well, you both know how well *that* turned out."

I giggled, remembering Leif and the Shoe Guy.

"I'm really happy for Aunt Joyce, but I'm a little sad, too," Erin went on. "I've always counted on being able to hang out with her after I graduate . . . she's so much fun, so free-wheeling. But now . . ." She trailed off.

"Do you think once Joyce is married things will change between you?" I asked.

Erin shot her empty straw wrapper across the

table. "I hope not. But guys always change everything, don't they?"

We nodded. They did.

I felt a nervous twinge as I remembered my essay. I decided to keep quiet about it and surprise my friends.

"So how's it going at home?" Kerri asked me. I'd told everyone the saga of my dad and Marlene.

"Nothing new. I haven't talked to my dad yet," I said. "But I think it's going to be okay."

"So are you going to talk to him today?" Erin asked.

"Definitely," I said, resolved. "The sooner the better."

By giving that essay to Alex, I'd finally done the right thing when it came to T.J. and to my rep at school.

Now I had to do the right thing with my father.

A light drizzle was coming down when I pulled into my driveway that afternoon. As I walked up the front sidewalk, I was surprised to see the parlor light shining through the windows. The parlor was my mom's sanctuary. Once she died, the room became off limits. Neither my dad nor I ever went in there. It was sad really; the parlor was probably the nicest room in the house: it had lots of windows and was full of some of my mom's favorite things.

I let myself in, shrugging out of my raincoat and sticking my umbrella in the porcelain holder. Then, curious, I headed toward the parlor. A thin band of light spilled out onto the hallway carpet. Tentatively I pushed open the door. It was just as I had remembered it. Tiny embroidered pillows littered the couch and varying patterns of chintz draped the walls, couch, and chairs. Except what I didn't remember ever seeing before was my dad sitting in one of those chairs, as he was tonight, with one of our family scrapbooks open on his lap.

My mom used to make big photo scrapbooks of everything: vacations, Thanksgiving family dinners, my field hockey games, you name it. I used to help her choose the pictures and paste them in.

My dad didn't look up as I entered, or when I walked over to stand next to him. His fingers were moving over a photograph of me and Mom outside Buckingham Palace the year before she died. "Remember our trip to England?" he asked, laughing softly to himself. "Your mom was determined to get one of the palace guards to laugh."

"And she did it, too," I recollected, smiling at the memory. "Of course she had to tell twelve stupid jokes before it worked, but she did it!"

Then, silence. I didn't know what to say to him,

and I had the feeling he felt exactly the same way.

Finally my dad cleared his throat. "I read your journal, Maya."

"I figured," I said, my palms sticky. "From your note."

"I'm so sorry I failed you." My dad looked up at me. He shook his head. "I just didn't know."

"You couldn't have," I whispered. "But you could have tried to find out."

"I guess I spent too much time wondering how I could be both a mother and a father to you and ended up not being either," he said.

"I didn't give you the journal to make you feel bad," I told him. "I did it so you could see who I am as a person." Our eyes met. "And I wasn't very honest either. I'm sorry, Dad."

"I love you, sweetheart," he whispered, tears filling his eyes. "And I know you think I'm over-protective, but it's just because I love you so much. I can't bear the thought of anything happening to you. I already lost your mother. I can't lose you too."

I flung myself into his arms. "You're never going to lose me," I said, my voice muffled. I pulled away a little. "So where does Marlene fit in all this?"

"Marlene and I have been working side by side for months. And somehow our relationship evolved into a romance." He rubbed his temples. "I wanted to tell you, but I was afraid of how you'd react. I could never, ever replace your mother, and I'd never want to. But I know your mom would want me to be happy, and being with Marlene makes me feel alive again." His face actually lit up. "She makes me laugh, Maya. She makes me think."

"Oh," I said again. I mean, what could I say to that? I hated the thought of him being involved with a woman other than my mom. But I owed it to him to try to be open-minded. My mother was gone, but my dad and I, we were still here. And she would have wanted us to live our lives to the fullest.

"You know, Maya, the way I've handled things lately hasn't been very smart," my dad admitted. "But again, I was only looking out for you. I wasn't sure you were old enough to handle my having a relationship."

"Dad, I'm going to be turning seventeen before you know it!" I exclaimed.

He smiled. "I know. I guess I didn't want to think about that yet."

I blinked. "So . . . are you okay with me seeing Luke?"

He nodded. "But once the campaign trail cools down I plan to spend a lot more time at home, so watch out," he warned, grinning.

He took my hands in his. "Maya, my work is

important to me. And it involves a lot of hours. I'm never going to be the kind of father who attends all your school events or is here sitting reading the paper when you come home from school. But I can promise you that I love you and care for you and will be the best father I know how to be."

I grinned back. "Sounds good to me."

# *Chapter 24*

The following article appeared in the Tuesday afternoon edition of the *Spectrum*:

### *Notes from the Threshold*

When you're a senior in high school, people tell you you're on the brink of something new. Big changes are coming. You're about to grow up. For us, as seniors, it's hard to see the difference between teens and adults. We've got one foot in childhood and one foot out the door. We're mixed up and torn in half. We think we're invincible, that nothing bad can ever happen to us. We can't imagine that anyone we know could die or that we ourselves could get hurt.

I used to have a plan of what my life was going to be like—and of course it was going to be perfect. Why wouldn't it? I had great parents, cool friends, good grades, and all the things money could buy. I had no reason to suspect that my world was about to shatter into a million pieces.

When my mother died from cancer, I couldn't believe it. It was *my* mom—not some random woman on a TV talk show or some other girl's mom from school. Mine. Before, when bad things happened to other people I'd tell them how sorry I was. But really, it was *their* lives that were affected, not mine. My perfect existence went on.

But all that changed. After the funeral I kept all my feelings bottled up. On the outside I was the same Maya, but inside I was sad, depressed, and angry. Angry that my mother could be taken away—just like that. Angry with my father too, who didn't make the hurt disappear. But he was grieving so much himself that he couldn't even see my pain.

I thought that maybe having a boyfriend to talk to would help. Someone to share things with. Someone who could make me laugh. Someone I could trust. That's when I learned that you can't trust everybody, and I found out what growing up really means.

Something happened to me this year that I never imagined in my worst nightmares. A boy I thought I could trust sexually assaulted me at a party. This was someone who walks the halls of

South Central every day.

Even after it happened, I could hardly believe it. Suddenly the world seemed scary. If I wasn't safe at a party with friends, where *could* I feel safe? I was afraid to come to school because the boy who assaulted me was here. He was spreading rumors about me—lies. And some people believed him. Sometimes it seemed as if the whole world had turned against me. My life was spiraling out of control.

I wanted to crawl into bed and never come out. But deep inside me I had a reserve of strength I never knew was there. I found the courage to face what happened to me, and found the courage to get help. I didn't let my problems crush me, and once I moved beyond them, a whole new world opened up. Not the safe protected world I'd once known, but not the dangerous place I was afraid of either.

It's a world without my mother to lean on and a world that's far from perfect. But it's also a place where support exists and friends care. A world I'm finally ready to be part of. I know now that you can't control the trauma in your life, but your reaction is your power.

Deal with your issues. Learn from them. Use your power.

There are still things that I can't believe are happening in my life. I can't believe the strength I feel now when I remember my mother. I can't believe the strong bond my father and I are forming as we live each day without her. I can't believe how empowered I feel, having survived the attack. How brave it was to find the help I needed to get through it.

You know what I *do* believe? I believe we're all on the threshold of a new existence that is both exciting and frightening. But we can't let our fears stop us from moving on. It takes courage to make that first step, but we all have the strength inside us. We just have to be ready to find it.

*Maya Christina Greer*

As I sat in homeroom and read my words in black and white, I wasn't sure anymore that I'd done the right thing. The whole embarrassing truth was right there for everyone to see.

But as the day wore on, I found out that it was the right thing, after all.

Melissa Klein came up to me in the hall after first period. "You were so brave to confront T.J. like that," she told me.

"I never said it was—"

She put her hand on my arm. "Maya, everyone

knows who you were talking about. Especially me. T.J. did the same thing to me last year, but the rumors weren't as bad." She smiled wryly. "Guess he was just getting warmed up."

And that was how it went throughout the day. Girls I knew and girls I didn't kept coming up to congratulate me. People were dissing T.J. and coming to my defense. Instead of making nasty comments in the halls, they were saying, "You tell him, Maya!" and "You go, girl!"

I was going into English class when Jimmy Wright stopped me in the hall. "Hey, Maya," Jimmy said. "I, uh, I just wanted to tell you that I'm sorry I've been kind of a jerk to you lately."

I shrugged, feeling awkward. I hadn't expected T.J.'s friends to get the message.

By the end of the day, I was almost walking on air. And then I saw T.J. striding down the hall in my direction.

*Oh, no,* I thought. My palms began to sweat, and my happy mood dissolved. *He's going to say something mean to me—I just know it. Just stay calm,* I told myself. *Don't let him know you're nervous.*

As he drew nearer, I braced myself for some kind of insult. He had to be upset about my essay. Everybody in school knew it was about him.

He stopped in front of me. Our eyes met. I forced

myself not to look away. I forced myself to stand firm.

T.J. opened his mouth, then let it fall shut. His eyes darted to the floor. Then he slinked off down the hall, head hanging down. He didn't look back.

*Ha!* I thought. A feeling of triumph surged through my body. Now *he* was afraid of *me*! The cloud that had been hovering over me was gone.

"Maya!" Jessica came racing down the hall. "You are *so* brave. What a great essay! I'm so proud of you. You really did it!"

"Thanks," I told her. "Your support really helped."

Jessica's hair was loose and wavy around her face, and her eyes had a sparkle in them. "You look great today, Jess," I said. "Is something up?"

Jessica smiled. "I hope." Her voice dropped to a whisper. "I think Alex and I might be getting back together!"

"Really? That's great!"

"Talking to him at the bowling alley was the first step. We e-mailed yesterday, and there was a note in my locker from him this morning. I think he misses me just as much as I miss him." She rocked back and forth on her toes. "If Alex and I are lucky enough to get together again, I will never, ever let him go."

"Hey, Maya." I turned around to see Luke

standing there, a folded copy of the *Spectrum* in his hand. He gave me a hug. "You didn't tell me about T.J. Are you okay?"

Jessica waved. "Gotta run. See ya!"

I shrugged. "I just wrote how I felt. Now I feel a lot better."

"I'm glad," Luke said. Then he smiled at me. "You look nice today, Maya."

"Thanks." I was wearing plaid jeans, a pink top, and small jeweled barrettes that Erin had helped me pick out—a look that was kind of funky for me.

"Maya, I want things to be cool with your dad," Luke said, taking my hand and lacing his fingers with mine. "I really want to keep seeing you, but I don't want to sneak around." His mouth was set in a determined line; it was really quite cute. "If your dad can't accept me, well, then . . ."

I squeezed his hand. "Are you free now?"

He nodded.

"I want you to meet him—I mean, actually talk to him this time," I said, grinning.

"Really?"

I nodded. "Really."

"Great." Luke looked pleased and a little nervous. "Are you sure? This isn't a trick?"

"I'm sure," I said.

We started down the hall toward the exit, and I

decided that my senior year would really begin from this point. Because I knew that the memories I was going to make from that day on were going to be good ones.

As we made our way through the crowded corridors of South Central, my eyes fell on a couple leaning against the lockers, kissing. The guy was tall, with an athletic build, and the girl was petite and brunette, wearing jeans and a green shirt.

My breath caught in my throat as I watched them pull away. It was Alex and Gretchen. *How am I going to tell Jessica about this?* I wondered. *It's going to crush her.*

Farther down the hall, I spotted Erin facing a row of lockers, searching through her backpack. "Be right back," I told Luke, and raced over there. "Erin. I have to talk to you. I just saw . . ." My voice trailed off when I caught sight of her tear-stained face. She had obviously been crying. "Erin, what's wrong? What happened?" I asked.

Erin quickly wiped her eyes with her hand. "Forget it. I don't want to talk about it." She zipped up her backpack.

"But I'm worried," I said. "You never cry. It must be something big."

"I told you I don't want to talk about it," Erin replied. "Look. I've got to get backstage," she said heading off. "I'll call you later. Okay?"

As I watched her rush away, a sick feeling spread through my stomach. I had to find out what was wrong with Erin. *It's not fair,* I thought. *Good things were finally happening in my life. Why couldn't it be that way for my friends too?*

# Here's a sneak peek at

# TURNING
## seventeen #4

## *Show Me Love*
### *Erin's Story*

*One sheep jumped over the fence. Two sheep jumped over the fence. Three sheep jumped over the fence.* This wasn't working. Instead of feeling sleepy, I found myself wondering why the singular of "sheep" was the same as the plural. For that matter, I wasn't convinced that a sheep could jump over a fence.

I had gotten home over an hour ago, but I still couldn't fall asleep. Even though I had turned off all of the lights in the house, I could still make out almost everything in the living room. Moonlight streamed in through Joyce's sliding glass doors, casting crazy shadows over the tables, lamps, and chairs.

I shifted on the sofa bed, trying to find a more comfortable position. In the months since I had left Aunt Joyce's, I had forgotten how many springs on this mattress were bent out of shape. It sort of felt like I was sleeping on a set of tools. And right now there was screwdriver digging into my spine.

*You're avoiding the issue, Erin,* I told myself. I wasn't really bothered by the spring coils. I was simply thinking about anything I could to avoid thinking about Keith—and the rest of my life.

But it was no use. No matter what thought came into my head, it inevitably brought me back to Keith. For instance, sheep made me think of wool, which made me think of the gray wool sweater I had borrowed from Keith last summer when we hiked Mount Ranier.

I decided to tally up the good signs and bad signs from the evening. Maybe if I analyzed the data, I would feel like I knew what was going on between us.

Dinner reservations at C & O Trattoria. *Good sign.* Initial peck on the lips. *Bad sign.* He was wearing what looked like a new shirt. *Good sign.* He didn't hold my hand in the car. *Bad sign.* Laughing about the Rose Lady. *Good sign.* Sharing our entrees. *Good sign.* Lingering for dessert. *Good sign.* Lukewarm goodnight kiss. *Bad sign. Major bad sign.*

There were more good signs than bad, but it seemed to me that the bad ones were so bad that it all equaled out. If only I knew what Keith was thinking and feeling. Was he lying in his bed dreaming about me at this very moment?

*Everything was so simple last summer,* I thought. It was as if Keith and I were the only two people who existed. We'd seen each other every day and every night. Life had been about picnics, swimming, concerts, dinners out, and parties. But now . . . now that seemed changed somehow.

Maybe, in the end, I was just a summer fling for Keith. A brief romance that had evaporated with summer. It was possible that Keith was even bummed that I was in town. Like he regarded me the same way he would a visiting great-aunt or second cousin. A duty.

But Keith had told me how excited he was to be my date to Aunt Joyce's wedding. He had said he "wouldn't miss it." Unless . . . unless Keith was just being nice. Maybe he didn't want to go with me at all.

I would hate it if Keith was just hanging out with me out of pity. It would be the most humiliating thing I could imagine! Just thinking about it made a hard knot form in the pit of my stomach.

I started to shift on the sofa, desperate to find one patch of the mattress that was at least semi-comfortable. As I moved, I noticed a dark shadow outside of the sliding glass doors.

Immediately, my heart started to pound—not the excited kind of pounding, but the scared kind. Outside, the shadow moved.

I slid off of the sofa bed and pulled on my sweat pants. Then I grabbed the portable phone. I wanted to be ready to dial 911 at a moment's notice.

I tiptoed toward the glass doors, praying that

exhaustion was making my mind play tricks on me. Me getting murdered two days before Aunt Joyce's wedding would put a serious damper on the festivities. Mom would never forgive me.

I stood at the edge of the doors and peered out into the moonlit night. There was the shadow! It had moved again, much closer this time. It's definitely a person, I realized.

The shadow moved closer . . . and closer. I flipped over the phone in my trembling had and pushed 9 and then 1.

"Erin?" The shadow spoke. "Erin, is that you?"

With my thumb, I hung up the phone. "Keith?" I whispered, sliding the glass door open a few inches.

The shadow emerged from behind a bush. It was Keith. "What's going on?" I whispered, opening the door wider to let him inside. "Why are you back here?"

Keith stepped inside, stopping just inches from me. "I forgot something."

"You did?" Having Keith so close was doing funny things to my stomach.

"Yeah." He put his hands on my waist and drew me even closer.

And then he kissed me. Not a small peck, but a knee-buckling, spine-tingling real kiss.

"Erin, it's been so long," Keith murmured against my ear. "I've missed you."

"I've missed you too," I whispered back, lifting my face to kiss him again.

We stood next to the door for what felt like hours, and I wished more than ever that we didn't have to say goodnight. Finally, Keith pulled away.

"I've got to go." He gave me another hard, quick kiss, then slipped out the door and waved good-bye.

I watched Keith retreat into the night until he disappeared. Once I heard his VW start, I closed the sliding glass doors and went back to my sofa bed.

As I closed my eyes, I felt like I was on cloud nine. But I also felt more confused than ever. Why hadn't Keith kissed me like that earlier in the evening? Why had he been holding back?

*Love is not like a romance novel,* I thought, drifting off to sleep. But one thing was definite. I wasn't going to have any problem falling asleep now.

### Don't miss the chance to win a trip to New York City and hang out with the editors of your favorite magazine!

## GRAND PRIZE

- 3-day, 2-night trip to New York City
- Meeting with the editors of seventeen
- Fabulous makeover at a New York City salon

## 3 FIRST PRIZES

- Personal astrological readings

## 50 SECOND PRIZES

- Cool makeup bags filled with makeup

---

### ENTER TO WIN

**Fill out and mail to:** HarperCollins Seventeen Sweepstakes
P.O. Box 8188
Grand Rapids, MN 55745-8188

_____

Name

_____

Date of Birth

_____

Parent/Legal Guardian (required if under 18)

_____

Address

_____

Address

_____

Phone

**One entry per person. No purchase necessary.
You must be between the ages of 13 and 21 to enter.
See back for official rules.**

# Seventeen Sweepstakes Official Rules

NO PURCHASE NECESSARY. SWEEPSTAKES OPEN ONLY TO LEGAL U.S. RESIDENTS BETWEEN THE AGES OF 13 AND 21 YEARS AS OF 9/1/00. Employees (and their immediate families and those living in their same households) and all officers, directors, representatives, and agents of HarperCollins Publishers, Parachute Properties, **seventeen** magazine, and any of their affiliates, parents, subsidiaries, advertising and promotion and fulfillment agencies are not eligible. Sweepstakes starts 9/1/00, and ends on 1/1/01. By participating, entrants agree to these official rules.

To Enter: Entries will be used by HarperCollins only for purposes of this Sweepstakes. Hand print your name, complete street address, city, state, zip, and phone number on this official entry form or on a 3 x 5 card and send to: HarperCollins Seventeen Sweepstakes, PO Box 8188, Grand Rapids, MN 55745-8188. Limit one entry per person/family/household. One entrant per entry. HarperCollins Publishers is not responsible for lost, miscommunicated, late, damaged, incomplete, stolen, misdirected, illegible, or postage-due mail entries. Entry materials/data that have been tampered with, altered, or that do not comply with these rules are void. Entries become the property of HarperCollins Publishers Inc., and will not be returned or acknowledged. Entries must be postmarked by 1/1/01, and received no later than 1/8/01.

Drawing: Winners will be selected in a random drawing held on or about 1/9/01 by HarperCollins Publishers, whose decisions are final, from all eligible entries received. Winners will be notified by mail on or about 1/15/01. The prizes will be awarded in the name of minor's parent or legal guardian. Odds of winning depend on total number of eligible entries received.

Prizes: Grand Prize: One (1) Grand Prize Winner will receive a trip to New York City for two (2) people (winner and parent or legal guardian) for 3 days, 2 nights at a date to be determined in Spring 2001. Prize consists of round-trip coach class air transportation to and from winner's nearest served airport (U.S. citizens residing in the U.S. at the time of the trip), standard hotel accommodations for one room, two nights, a day with the editors of **seventeen** magazine, and a makeover at a New York City salon to be chosen by sponsor. Total approximate retail value (ARV) is $3,000.00. Travel/accommodation restrictions may apply. All other expenses not specifically stated are the sole responsibility of the winner. Winner must travel with winner's parent/legal guardian if winner is a minor in his/her state of residence. Travel and use of accommodation are at risk of winner and parent/legal guardian and HarperCollins, Parachute, and **seventeen** magazine do not assume any liability. First-place prize: 3 First Place Prize winners will each receive a personal astrological reading by an astrologer chosen by sponsor, the time and place to be determined at sponsor's sole discretion. Approximate retail value (ARV) is $500.00 each. Second-place Prize: 50 Second Prize Winners will each receive a special makeup bag filled with makeup. Approximate retail value (ARV) is $10.00 each. Total value of all prizes is $5,000.00. In the event Grand Prize Winner is unable to travel/accept prize during time specified, Grand Prize Winner shall be considered to have irrevocably forfeited prize and an alternate Grand Prize Winner will be selected. If any prize is not available or cannot be fulfilled, HarperCollins, Parachute, and **seventeen** magazine reserve the right to substitute a prize of equal or greater value. Prizes are not redeemable for cash value by winners.

General Conditions: By taking part in this Sweepstakes entrants agree to be bound by these official rules and by all decisions of HarperCollins Publishers, Parachute Publishing, and **seventeen** magazine. Winners or their parents/legal guardians, if minor in his/her state of residence, are required to sign and return an Affidavit of Eligibility and Liability Release and where legal, a Publicity Release within ten (10) days of notification. Failure to return documents as specified, or if prize notification or prize is returned as nondeliverable, may result in prize forfeiture and selection of an alternate winner. Grand Prize Winner and his/her travel companion must sign and return a Liability/Publicity Release prior to issuance of travel documents. Sweepstakes is subject to all applicable federal, state, and local laws and regulations and is void in Puerto Rico and wherever else prohibited by law. By participating, winners (and winners parents/legal guardians) agree that HarperCollins Publishers, Parachute, **seventeen** magazine, and their affiliate companies, parents, subsidiaries, advertising and promotion agencies, and all of their respective officers, directors, employees, representatives, and agents will have no liability whatsoever, and will be held harmless by all winners (and winners' parents/legal guardians, if applicable) for any liability for any injuries, losses, or damages of any kind to person, including death, and property resulting in whole or in part, directly or indirectly, from the acceptance, possession, misuse, or use of the prize, or participation in this Sweepstakes. Except where legally prohibited, by accepting prize, winners (and winners' parents/legal guardians, as applicable) grant permission for HarperCollins Publishers, Parachute, **seventeen** magazine, and those acting under their authority to use his/her name, photograph, voice and/or likeness, for advertising and/or publicity purposes without additional compensation. Taxes on prizes are solely the responsibility of the winners. Prizes are not transferable and cannot be assigned.

Prize Winners' Names: For the names of the Winners (available after 1/15/01), send a self-addressed stamped envelope for receipt by 1/31/01 to HarperCollins Seventeen Sweepstakes, PO Box 8105, Grand Rapids, MN 55745-8105.

Sponsored by HarperCollins Publishers, New York, NY 10019-4703.

# *seventeen*